ASK THE
Bones

ASK THE
Bones

Scary Stories from
Around the World

selected and retold
by Arielle North Olson
and Howard Schwartz

illustrated by David Linn

Viking

VIKING
Published by the Penguin Group
Penguin Putnam Books for Young Readers, 345 Hudson Street, New York,
New York 10014, U.S.A.
Penguin Books Ltd, 27 Wrights Lane, London W8 5TZ, England
Penguin Books Australia Ltd, Ringwood, Victoria, Australia
Penguin Books Canada Ltd, 10 Alcorn Avenue, Toronto, Ontario, Canada
M4V 3B2
Penguin Books (N.Z.) Ltd, 182–190 Wairau Road, Auckland 10, New Zealand

Penguin Books Ltd, Registered Offices: Harmondsworth, Middlesex, England

First published in 1999 by Viking, a member of Penguin Putnam Books
for Young Readers.

1   3   5   7   9   10   8   6   4   2

LIBRARY OF CONGRESS CATALOGING-IN-PUBLICATION DATA
Ask the bones: scary stories from around the world / selected and retold by
Arielle North Olson and Howard Schwartz ; illustrated by David Linn.
p.   cm.
Includes bibliographical references (p.   ).
Summary: A collection of scary folktales from countries around the world
including China, Russia, Spain, and the United States.
ISBN 0-670-87581-3
1. Horror tales.   2. Tales.   [1. Horror stories.   2. Folklore.]
I. Olson, Arielle North.   II. Schwartz, Howard, date.   III. Linn, David, ill.
PZ8.1.A826   1999   398.27–dc21   98-19108   CIP   AC

Printed in U.S.A.
Set in Caslon 540 Roman

Contents

Contents (continued)

Introduction

Since ancient times, the night has seemed mysterious and threatening. Shadows beyond the firelight gave rise to tales as frightening as our worst nightmares. These stories account for more shivers than the most chilling wind.

The scary folktales gathered in this book come from around the world—from the United States, China, Russia, Spain, and other far-off lands.

Here ghostly pirates take unspeakable revenge on those who dare to dig for their treasure, and witches turn unfortunate men into oxen whenever they please. Here the devil bargains for souls, a kindly cousin turns out to have a grisly appetite, and evil eyes endanger the unsuspecting.

It is only human to tremble at the unknown, especially after dark, when you don't know if you are hearing branches rubbing against the window or evil creatures prowling around outside your door.

The ones who lurk within these pages are lying in wait for you . . . so take care.

ASK THE
Bones

The Haunted Forest

Long ago there was a haunted forest in Uzbekistan. No one who stepped into its shadows was ever seen again.

Rusty axes lay on the ground, dropped there by wood-cutters who disappeared forever. Baskets lay smashed in the bushes, left by terrified berry pickers who never returned home.

The roaring was terrible. It echoed through the forest day and night. But what roared? No one knew.

Some said that evil spirits waited in the gloom, ready to pounce upon their victims and lock them deep inside the trunks of trees. Why else did the branches moan in the wind?

Others said that monsters with dozens of long hairy arms rose up through the forest floor and pulled their victims

1

deep beneath the earth, leaving only the axes and baskets behind.

The Khan told everyone that neither evil spirits nor hairy monsters lurked in the forest, only a mighty beast. A hungry beast. A beast who could eat an entire man for dinner, yet roar its displeasure if it didn't find a tender maiden for dessert.

The Khan wanted someone to slip into the forest and kill this beast. He was sure he could find a man brave enough to do it. And if that man disappeared forever, the Khan wouldn't worry. He could always find others, particularly if he offered a prize.

So the Khan issued a proclamation. "Let it be known," the proclamation stated, "that a great prize will be given to whoever kills the beast in the forest and brings back its head."

Hunters came, who could spear a sapling at fifty paces, cleanly splitting it in two.

Soldiers came, who could slice their swords through the air faster than the eye could see.

But one by one they disappeared into the forest. Peasants living nearby heard hideous screams amidst the roaring. And they never saw the brave men again.

The peasants piled chairs and tables against their doors at night so nothing from the forest could burst into their huts. They spoke softly to one another, not knowing who or what might be listening. "Only a fool would attempt to win the prize," some whispered.

But the shoemaker's son decided to try.

His name was Hasan, and he had heard about evil spirits and monsters ever since he was a child. At bedtime, when dark shadows filled the hut, his mother had told him stories that set his imagination on fire. A cloak hanging on a peg seemed alive when the wind blew through a crack in the wall. Pots and pans looked like heads that had dropped down the chimney and were sitting on the hearth, waiting to devour him as soon as he closed his eyes.

As he grew older, cloaks and pots and pans looked familiar, except when he awoke in the dark, still immersed in his dreams.

But the frightful roaring in the forest? He never got used to that. It made his skin creep and his scalp tingle. Still, he tended to believe the Khan. It was just a beast. And what beast, he thought, could not be outwitted by a man?

When Hasan turned sixteen, he announced he was going to win the Khan's prize. His mother and father feared for his life, but he promised to be careful. Finally they let him go to the Khan's palace.

Now the Khan had seen many men try and fail, so he was amused that a mere boy would attempt to kill such a ferocious beast. But he gave Hasan a helmet, a shield, and a sword.

Hasan thanked the Khan and hurried away. By the time he reached the haunted forest, night had fallen. He carried a flaming torch that lit up the path, but the circle of light made the surrounding woods seem much darker and far more dangerous.

Never before had Hasan ventured into the depths of the forest, and never at night. His torch made eerie shadows, and branches rubbed in the wind, rasping and groaning overhead. Hasan remembered hearing about evil spirits who trapped their victims within the trunks of trees. But he told himself he heard only the wind, nothing more. Still, he trembled.

Suddenly he heard a faint rustling in the dry leaves beside the path, and he remembered his mother's stories about hairy arms shooting up through the leaves to pull unwary travelers into the depths of the earth. Just stories? Then why was his heart pounding so?

He stopped, his eyes darting left and right. There was something very dark and very large looming ahead. He held his torch high, breathing fast, but he saw that it was merely the tumbledown wall of an old castle. He decided he would rather meet the beast in daylight, so he prepared to spend the night there, sheltered by the castle's remaining walls.

He gathered some wood and soon had a fire blazing. Its warmth made him drowsy, but just as he was closing his eyes he heard the rustling again. Was something rising up through the leaves on the forest floor? Then he heard a soft voice.

"I'm cold," it said. "May I sit by your fire?"

Hasan jumped up and held his sword ready. Could something monstrous be lurking there, making its voice sweet as honey?

Hairy arms slid around the end of the castle wall. Or were they hairy legs?

Hasan raised his sword high above his head, his hands trembling, ready to strike.

Whatever it was, it spoke again, even more gently than before. "Fear not," it said, "and do not believe what you are about to see. Although I look like a giant spider, I am really a girl."

A shiny black body, with the longest, hairiest legs Hasan had ever seen, scuttled into the circle of firelight. Was this one of the monsters his mother had warned him about?

Hasan gripped his sword even more tightly. But the spider stayed on the opposite side of the fire.

"One day my veil slipped," it said, "when an evil magician was passing by. He saw my face and wanted to marry me. So I ran. And that's when he called upon Suliman, son of David, the one who honors all requests, and turned me into a spider."

Hasan wanted to believe the spider, but he needed

5

proof. "Recite the evening prayer," he said, "if you truly are a person." And the spider spoke the words in its soft and gentle voice.

Hasan lowered his sword. "Maybe we can find something to release you from the spell," he said.

"And maybe I can help you," said the spider, "for I know why you are here." It moved close to Hasan, folded its long hairy legs and watched over him while he slept.

The next morning, Hasan was awakened by a hideous roar that made the very earth shudder. He and the spider leaped to their feet just as a monstrous lion jumped over the castle wall. It was ten times bigger than any lion on earth, with its ears laid back, tail lashing, and claws ready to cut them to bits.

And it could talk.

"Who dares trespass in my forest?" it roared. And before the amazed Hasan could draw his sword, the lion slammed him to the ground with one huge paw and pinned the spider's legs with another. "I eat all who enter here! I ate the woodsmen. I ate the berry pickers. I ate the soldiers. I ate the hunters and now . . ."

It opened its mouth wide and exposed its razor-sharp fangs.

"Wait, wait," cried Hasan. "Don't you want to hear the spider's story first?"

The mighty lion closed its mouth. "Perhaps," it said and lifted its paws.

The spider spoke so sadly about the life it had led since meeting the evil magician that the lion took pity on it. "Come to my cave," said the lion to the spider, "where I have some magic ointment. A sorcerer gave it to me in exchange for safe passage through my forest. Let's see what it will do."

So the monstrous lion led Hasan and the spider down into the depths of its cave. It pawed aside a pile of rocks and brought forth a small clay pot. Then the lion dipped a stick into the ointment and rubbed it on the spider's head. A cloud of smoke enveloped the spider. And when it swirled away, a veiled maiden stood before them, clothed in shimmering silk. (She was as lovely a girl as Hasan had ever seen. He was beside himself with joy.

So was the girl. "Thank you, dear lion," she cried. "I will be grateful to you forever."

But the lion was not listening. It lashed its tail and snarled ferociously. "I have always said people taste better than spiders—and two make a delicious meal."

It sprang toward them.

The girl threw the magic ointment at the lion.

Hasan swung his sword.

But who was the quickest?

Did Hasan cut off the lion's head and carry it to the palace? Were he and the girl rewarded with a magic carpet that flew them around the world?

8

Or did the girl fling the magic ointment in time to turn the lion into a kitten?

Or, horror of horrors, did the lion gobble up Hasan and the girl with a bloodcurdling *crunch?*

It all depends on whether the spots on this page are tears of joy or drops of blood . . . You decide!

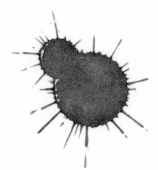

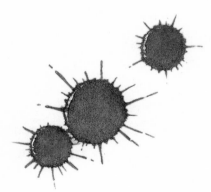

The Murky Secret

It appeared one day in 1867—a green glass bottle sitting on the druggist's counter. It was a huge bottle, but what amazed customers was the creature floating around inside.

Its face was grotesque, with wrinkled cheeks, staring eyes, and lips twisted into a hideous grin.

But its body was worse. It was shriveled, with hairy arms. And a fishlike tail hung where its legs should be.

"It's a pickled mermaid," said the druggist, his eyes glowing. "I bought it from a sailor."

The druggist's assistant shuddered. The boy had seen more than enough of his employer's ghastly specimens lined up in the back room, all floating in bottles of brine. A shrunken sea serpent with two heads. Something dredged

10

up from the depths of the ocean that was all spines and teeth. A gelatinous blob studded with bulging eyes.

And just this morning a new bottle had appeared on the highest shelf, a bottle identical to the one that enclosed the pickled mermaid. But the liquid was too murky for the boy to see what was inside.

Whatever it was, it fascinated the druggist. He often slipped into the back room to visit his newest specimen. And when he emerged, his sharp face was lit up by an evil grin. He looked like a thief who had just stolen a fortune in gold.

The druggist enjoyed having a pickled mermaid on his front counter. He watched his customers' faces and snorted with laughter when he saw their looks of horror and disgust.

One old woman tugged at the druggist's arm, pulling his head low so she could whisper in his ear. "You'll be sorry," she said. "Merfolk don't take kindly to anyone who harms them."

But the druggist just shrugged. He combed his fingers through his pointed goatee, separating the gray hairs in the center from the black ones on each side. "I fear nothing," he said. Then he smirked like someone relishing a secret.

But at that very moment, something happened that surprised even the druggist.

Suddenly the sun was eclipsed by a jet-black sky. Lightning flashed, thunder roared, and rain poured forth as if all the water on earth had risen to the heavens in order to fall upon this coastal city.

Never before had the residents of Charleston experienced such a furious storm. At night they pulled their pillows over their heads, shutting out the flashes of blinding light. But they could not escape the ear-splitting thunder. It rattled their beds and sent tremors of fear all the way down to their toes.

They desperately hoped the weather would change. But it did not. Night after night and day after day, the violent storm assaulted the city.

Evil-smelling water oozed into cellars. Yowling cats climbed onto roofs and into treetops. And inch by inch the water rose in the streets until it lapped at the steps of the druggist's store.

As the days dragged on, residents began to mutter. Surely there was a reason for such a storm.

The old woman who had warned the druggist began to roam the streets, crying out hysterically—"The merfolk are angry," she shrieked. "We'll all drown unless the mermaid is returned to the sea."

Down by the docks, the superstitious sailors agreed. They believed that merfolk controlled the weather, accompanying ships they liked through gentle seas and sending those they disliked into the teeth of violent storms.

"This flood is the druggist's fault," they said. "He's the one who has a pickled mermaid!"

The word spread from alley to alley, lane to lane. Soon residents were pouring out of their houses and marching toward the druggist's store. Wind raged, tearing at their clothes and whipping the neverending rain into their eyes. They slogged along the streets, knee-deep in mud, and at each crossing they were joined by others, fists raised and faces contorted by anger and fear.

By the time the mob arrived at the store, the druggist had sent his assistant to bolt the front door. The marchers were furious. They pounded on the door with their fists. "Give us your mermaid," they shouted. "Give us your mermaid if you value your life!"

The druggist raced upstairs and leaned out a second-story window. "I have no mermaid," he said. "It was only a trick."

"We saw her," someone shouted, and everyone began chanting, "We saw her."

"You're wrong," yelled the druggist, and he sent his assistant to get the bottle from the front counter.

The boy wrestled it up the stairs, and the druggist held it in front of the window. But before he could uncork it, a rock was flung by someone at the back of the crowd. It hit the bottle and shattered it. Now the druggist was angry. He kicked aside the broken glass with his brine-soaked shoes and picked up the slimy creature.

"You fools!" he said. "Watch." And he snipped at hidden stitches around its waist. When the two halves fell

13

free, he waved them in front of the crowd. "The bottom is the tail of a fish, the top is part of a monkey. I tricked you all."

This enraged the mob. Not only had they been fooled but the rain was still pouring down, and now they had no mermaid to throw back into the sea.

They picked up dead rats floating past their knees and hurled them at the druggist. "No one else in Charleston would capture a mermaid," a man shouted. "You must have one somewhere." And he threw a handful of mud that found its target.

The druggist backed away from the window, wiping the muck off his face, his eyes flashing.

More mud and stones thudded against the store. Windows broke, and a wooden panel in the front door splintered.

The druggist grabbed his assistant's arm. "Hurry! Save the bottle on the top shelf of the back room. Hide it for me. I'll delay the crowd."

The frightened boy raced down the stairs. He could hear the mob breaking through the front door, tossing medications about, trampling on dried herbs. He rushed into the back room. Twice the key slipped from his sweaty hands, but he finally managed to lock himself in. Then he pushed a ladder over to the shelves and grabbed the bottle of murky liquid.

When he tipped the bottle, he was startled to see a flash

of shimmering scales inside—and a lock of golden hair. Stranger yet, he thought he heard a muffled song rising and falling within, like waves lapping upon a moonlit beach.

By now the mob was pounding on the door to the back room. He heard the druggist bellowing above the roar of the crowd. "Just a dusty old storeroom," he shouted, but angry men were ramming the locked door with their shoulders.

The boy flung open a window to the alley, struggled to lower the bottle to the ground, and dove out headfirst. He was so muddy that he could barely hang onto the bottle. But he hugged it to his chest and floundered along as fast as he could. The mermaid pressed her face against the glass and smiled.

The boy was about to turn the corner and slip out of sight when he heard the mob crash into the back room. He looked and saw someone leaning out the open window. "There he goes," the man shouted, and he jumped out the window, followed by a dozen others. They rushed after him, splashing and yelling, sure that the bottle held the very mermaid they wanted to return to the sea.

The boy's legs were aching and he was breathing hard, but he forced himself to run faster.

Then one man began to pelt him with iron nails from his pocket, trying to break the bottle. He was a carpenter who thought that hitting a mermaid with iron would undo her spells.

By now the boy's heart was pounding in his ears. But he could still hear the mermaid's song. It made him forget everything the druggist had said. He would not hide that bottle even if he could escape from the mob. Nor would he let the carpenter or anyone else hurt her. He must return the mermaid to the ocean himself.

So he splashed down to the dock, tugged desperately at the bottle's cork, and pulled it free. At that very moment, the druggist raced past the mob like a man possessed. He leaped onto the dock. "Stop!" he screamed. But the boy was too quick. He flung the uncorked bottle into the water, mermaid and all.

Suddenly a giant wave crashed ashore. It split, as if sliced by a knife, and missed the boy. But it engulfed the druggist in a wall of water and sucked him to the bottom of the sea.

Then the sun began to shine.

Months later, when the boy was walking along the beach, he came upon the very bottle that had imprisoned the mermaid. He leaped back, horrified to see something dead and shriveled within.

Not the mermaid!

He forced himself to take a closer look. And when he rolled the bottle over, he shuddered. For inside was a shrunken corpse with a scraggly goatee, gray in the center and black on each side.

Next-of-Kin

The old man longed for children. But he and his young wife had none, so he invited his nephew to live with them. This infuriated his wife, who had a vile temper. When her husband welcomed the young man with great affection, she turned pale with jealousy. Her eyes narrowed and her head flattened.

And when she licked her lips, her nephew saw that her tongue was *forked*.

From that day on, the young man spent as much time as possible with his uncle and tried to avoid his aunt. But she seemed to enjoy startling him, suddenly appearing when he least expected her.

One evening, the nephew returned to the house quite late. He lit a candle and started up the stairs. Halfway up, he tripped on what seemed to be a coiled rope. Imagine his horror when that rope uncoiled and slithered up the steps in front of him! Then he saw it glide across the hall and under the door of his uncle's bedroom.

"Wake up! Wake up!" the young man shouted, and he knocked on the door until his knuckles hurt. But when his sleepy uncle finally let him in the bedroom, there was no snake in sight.

His aunt seemed to be sleeping, so the young man whispered in his uncle's ear, "I saw a snake." But his uncle was too groggy to respond, and he slid back under the covers. The young man searched the room quietly, looking into drawers and cupboards and corners. He peered under the bed and behind chairs. He was beginning to think he was going mad when suddenly his aunt sat up in bed, narrowed her eyes, and gave him an evil look that made his flesh creep.

"I'm sorry to bother you," he cried, racing to his bedroom and firmly shutting the door.

When he awoke the next morning, he noticed that the bottom of his bedroom door was arched up in the center, leaving just enough space for a snake to slither through. He bolted out of bed trembling.

When he went downstairs, he was shocked to see that every door in the house had a snake-sized arch beneath it.

His aunt was sitting at the table, eating. "Your uncle left for the day," she said, licking her lips with her forked tongue. The young man was too terrified to speak, but his silence only made matters worse.

"I don't like the way you treat me," she said and grabbed his arm. Then she pressed her fingernails so deeply into his skin that he felt as if he were being bitten. He rushed outdoors and saw that his arm was swelling. His hand and fingers were beginning to throb.

He knew he must seek help, so he ran into the forest to find the wise old hermit who lived there. The old man examined him carefully and handed him some leaves. "These are best for snakebite," he said. "Bind them around your arm and keep them wet."

"But I wasn't bitten by a snake," said the young man. "Those marks were made by my aunt's fingernails."

The old hermit shook his head in despair. "The touch of a snake-woman is even worse," he said, "but try these leaves. They should help."

The young man was appalled. "Is my aunt really a snake-woman?" he asked.

"If you want to find out," the hermit replied, "stay awake tonight, and if a snake enters your room, cut off the tip of its tail."

The young man wasn't sure how this would help, but he thanked the hermit for his advice and returned to his uncle's house. By afternoon, he was happy to see that the wet leaves had reduced the swelling.

He watched his aunt closely that evening, but he didn't

notice anything strange until she tasted her soup. She said it needed more "ssssseasoning" and lingered on the *s* as if she were hissing. Her nephew felt gooseflesh rise from the tips of his toes to the top of his head. He excused himself from the table and went up to his bedroom.

But not to sleep.

He planned to watch for the snake all night long. There was just enough moonlight for him to see the bottom of his door, so he blew out his candle and unsheathed his sword. Then he stood waiting.

He watched for hours wondering what the snake might do. What if it slithered through the window instead, crept up behind him, and struck him with its venomous fangs? What if it slithered to the top of the wardrobe and dropped down on him from above? He was thinking of fleeing for his life, when he finally saw the snake glide under the door—first its head, then its body, then its tail.

Slash! He swung his sword so quickly that the snake had no warning. And the tip of its tail began writhing, all by itself, there on the floor.

The snake raised its head as if to strike, but then it hissed viciously and slithered out of the room. And when he looked down the hall, he saw it disappear under his uncle's door.

The young man couldn't stand looking at that quivering tail, so he scooped it up with his sword and flung it in a drawer. He hardly slept all that night, and when he did, snakes chased him through his dreams.

The next morning, he opened the drawer a crack to look at the snake's tail and was amazed to see that it had turned into human toes.

He raced back to the forest to tell the hermit what had happened. "And now my aunt is staying in bed, but do you know what my uncle said? She told him she hurt her foot while *sleepwalking*!"

"Either she will fear you now," said the old man. "Or she will try to get rid of you. Listen carefully. If you think you are in danger, you must search her bedroom for her snakeskin, and when you find it, burn it."

The young man thanked the hermit, but he was concerned. What would happen if he burned the snakeskin? He decided to give his aunt one last chance.

While she was recovering, she caused no trouble, but as soon as her wound healed, she resumed her nightly slithering about the house.

Sometimes, when the young man was lying in bed, he saw the snake slip in and out of his empty boots or up the sleeve of a coat he had worn. One dreadful night, he felt the snake wiggling under his pillow, and he jumped out of bed in a cold sweat.

His dreams grew worse. He had a terrifying nightmare in which his aunt was trying to choke him. He awoke gasping for breath and realized that something was coiled tightly around his neck.

It was the snake.

He pulled it off and threw it across the room. And after he caught his breath, he knew he had to follow the hermit's advice.

The next day his aunt said her back was sore, but this didn't keep her from going for a walk with his uncle. As soon as they left the house, the young man slipped into their bedroom to look for the snakeskin, but he couldn't find it. He was about to give up when he noticed dusty footprints on a chair. He stepped up on the seat and looked on top of the wardrobe, and there, neatly coiled, lay the shiny snakeskin.

But just as he picked it up, he heard the door open downstairs, and he knew that his aunt and uncle were home. He rolled up the snakeskin tightly and hid it in his fist before he raced back to his room. And that's when he heard hideous sounds coming from the lower hall.

His aunt was shrieking, "Something is crushing me!"

When her nephew heard her cries, he almost lost his resolve. But then he remembered how he felt when the snake wrapped itself around his neck and tried to choke him.

He threw the snakeskin into the fire and watched it burn.

By the time he went downstairs, he was startled to see his aunt lying dead on the floor. He thought he was getting rid of the snake, but now his aunt was gone too.

"I'm sorry," he said to his uncle.

But the old man seemed relieved. "It'ssss only the poisonousssss onessssss who are dangeroussssssss," he said, and he licked his lips.

The Bloody Fangs

Long ago, there was a boy in Japan who wished he were as strong as his brothers. They could work alongside their father planting rice. They could jump and run and climb trees.

The boy could not. He was small for his age and he tired easily. But he had a lively mind and filled his lonely hours drawing.

The boy's family was poor and had no money for paper and ink, so he used whatever he could find. He sharpened sticks and scratched pictures in the dirt. He gathered pieces of charcoal and drew upon smooth stones.

And what did he draw? Cats. Cats lashing their tails and cats washing their ears, cats stalking mice and cats leaping into the air.

His brothers wanted him to draw goblins with hideous eyes and great sharp fangs, but the boy never drew anything but cats.

The boy's parents realized he wasn't strong enough to become a farmer, so they decided he should become a priest. And why not? Even poor boys could hope to devote their lives to the service of Buddha.

One morning, the mother and father walked down to the village temple with their small son. They stood before the door and listened to the prayers being chanted inside by the old priest. They waited until the chanting stopped. Then they knocked.

The priest came to the door and asked what he could do for them. They told him they wanted the boy to become his student. The old man smiled. He would enjoy teaching such a bright and eager boy, so he invited him to live at the temple.

The boy tried hard to think right and speak right and do right. He learned to recite important prayers, and he kept the temple free of dust—but he couldn't keep his mind on his studies.

He had to draw cats.

When the sun set and crickets chirped in the grove around the temple, the boy would open the writing box, grind ink, mix it with water, and draw. He could hear the voice of the old priest reading scriptures on the other side of the temple, accompanied by the tinkling of bells. The boy knew he should be studying, but his hands could not be stilled. He drew cats everywhere, even on the walls and on the floor.

The priest was not pleased.

"You have an excellent mind," he told the boy. "You could learn everything a priest needs to know. But I cannot keep you as my student. Your heart is in your drawing. You must become an artist.

"But take my advice," the man said. "Avoid the large at night, keep to the small."

What did the priest mean? The boy was too upset to ask. Early the next morning he said good-bye and walked out the temple door.

He wanted to go home to his family, but what would his parents think? They expected him to follow the ways of Buddha. How could he tell them he had failed?

So he wandered down the road to the next village where there was a larger temple and more priests. Perhaps they would welcome a young student.

When he reached that temple, he was aware of a strange silence. No insects buzzed in the nearby bamboo grove. No temple bells rang. And there was no musical droning of voices from within.

The boy knocked at the door, but no one answered. He knocked again and the door swung slowly inward, so he stepped inside. He was amazed to see that the temple was filled with cobwebs and dust. "The priests need my help," he thought to himself. "I'll wait until they come back."

What he did not notice were the pawprints on the floor. Huge pawprints and the marks of sharp claws.

All he noticed were large white screens, set here and there in the temple. He hurried to the writing box. Never before had he seen such magnificent places on which to draw cats.

The hours flew past while he was drawing. Hundreds of cats now decorated the temple. Cats with every marking imaginable, contented cats and snarling cats, huge cats and newborn kittens.

It began to grow dark, and still no priests returned. The boy decided to spend the night there, hoping the priests would come back in the morning. He peered around the dim temple. It was the largest place he had ever seen. Suddenly he felt his hair stand on end.

"Avoid the large, keep to the small." That's what the old priest had said. What did the warning mean? The boy didn't know, but he hurried about looking for a small place—and safety.

It was growing so dark he could hardly see, but finally he found a small cupboard. At first he thought he couldn't squeeze in, but he wiggled through the opening, pulled his knees up to his chin, and just barely managed to pull the cupboard door shut.

There was a decorative grating in the cupboard door, a perfect peephole. He wanted to keep watch that night, but it was far too dark. Besides, he was tired, and before he knew it, he fell asleep.

He had barely closed his eyes when something quietly pushed open the temple door and crept inside. Its claws clicked across the floor and its nose swung this way and that, sniffing, sniffing, sniffing. It smelled boy! And it wanted boy for dinner.

It began to scratch at the cupboard door, hooking its claws in the grating, trying to pull it free.

The boy woke up to the wildest, screechiest battle he had ever heard. The whole temple was awash with shrieks and howls, the gnashing of teeth, the slashing of claws.

The boy couldn't see a thing through the grating on the cupboard door. So he squeezed his eyes shut and curled up even more tightly than before.

The terrible battle continued. Wetness splashed through the grating and onto his face. When the boy licked his lips, he thought he tasted *blood*.

It was almost more than he could stand. He now realized that his parents would have welcomed him home. They never would have wished such a terrifying night on their small son.

Just when he thought the howling and shrieking would never end, it stopped, just like that. And an eerie silence fell over the temple.

The boy didn't get another wink of sleep that entire night. When the sun finally rose, he peered through the grating in the cupboard door.

He could scarcely believe what he saw. There were great clumps of hair on the floor and blood was spattered everywhere. Scarier still was the monstrous carcass lying against the far wall. It was bigger than a cow and had the most hideous face the boy had ever seen—the face of a goblin rat.

Now the boy understood why the priests had fled from the temple.

But what on earth could have torn the goblin rat apart? The boy pushed open the cupboard door and crawled out. He rubbed his aching arms and legs and looked around. Except for the gory mess, everything in the temple looked just as it had the evening before.

Or did it?

The boy looked at the cats he had painted on the great white screens, and he saw that every mouth of every cat was stained with blood—the blood of the goblin rat.

Ask the Bones

Yusef had always avoided the man with cruel eyes who came to the outdoor market to hire young servants. But now the boy was desperate.

He could no longer run errands for the old woman who'd sold vegetables, because she had died. His coins were gone and his hunger pangs were unbearable.

Yusef watched the cruel man buying silk and spices at a nearby stand. And when the man took money from his pouch, two rubies tumbled out. The man quickly scooped them up.

But Yusef had seen them. Surely such a rich man could buy good food for his servants. Yusef tugged at the man's cloak.

"Well?" asked the man harshly.

"Could I work for you?" Yusef stammered.

"I can always use another boy," the man said. "But where's your family?"

"I have no family," said Yusef.

The man's eyes glinted more cruelly than before. "Come along, then." And he loaded all his purchases into the young boy's arms.

When they arrived at the man's home, he showed Yusef a place where he could sleep in the barn. At least the straw was soft, and there was a roof overhead.

The boy was given food each day, scraps, really, from his master's table. But to Yusef it was a feast. In return, he cared for the man's livestock—cows, calves, bulls, and camels.

The man had hired other boys before, but none lived there now. Yusef wondered where they'd found work.

All went well for almost a week. Then the man asked him to kill a bull and skin it. It was a miserable, bloody task, but Yusef gritted his teeth and did what he was told. And no sooner had he wiped the gore off his hands and face than his master ordered him to prepare two camels for a journey. "One for me and one to carry the hide of the bull."

Yusef thought they would travel to the outdoor market and sell the hide there. Instead they headed toward a wild and lonely plain. The boy grew more uneasy by the hour. He walked behind the camels with the sun beating down upon him. The stones were sharp underfoot. Up ahead, a

31

mountain rose like a needle into the sky. Its sides were incredibly steep, and there were no footholds in sight.

Yusef ran alongside the camel that was carrying his master. "Why do we need a bull's hide out here?" he asked.

"No questions," the man said. "Just do what I tell you." And his eyes looked colder than ever.

By the time they reached the base of the mountain, Yusef was sick with fear, and with good reason, for the man ordered him to spread the bull's smelly hide on the ground and lie on it.

The boy knew that the man was stronger than he was, so he squatted on the hide, ready to jump if necessary. But the man knocked him flat and tied the hide around him so quickly that Yusef hardly knew what was happening. Then the man hid behind a rock.

Within moments Yusef felt himself rising into the air, the hide clutched in the talons of a giant bird. He landed with a jolt on the mountaintop.

The bird began to rip off the remaining bits of the bull's flesh. It punctured the hide and raked its sharp beak across the boy's shoulder. He panicked. Kicking and punching, he fought his way out of the hide and frightened the bird away.

His legs were shaking, but he walked to the edge of the mountain and looked down.

"Hurry," the man shouted from below. "Throw me the gems that are around your feet."

The boy was amazed. Diamonds, rubies, and emeralds covered the ground. He threw them down by the handful.

The man grabbed some empty sacks from behind his saddle, filled them with gems, and laid them across one camel's back. Then he mounted the other camel and began to ride away.

"Wait!" cried Yosef. "How do I get down?"

"That's for you to figure out," shouted the man. "Don't ask me. Ask the bones." And off he went.

What bones?

The boy lay down, with his head over the edge of the mountain so he could peer at its sheer walls. He felt something hard beneath his chest. He dragged it out and stared at it with horror. It was a skull. A skull about the size of his own. He looked around and saw bones all over the mountaintop. There were leg bones and arm bones and finger bones and toe bones. And skulls everywhere. A few tears streamed down Yusef's cheeks. How many boys had the cruel man abandoned there? And how long would it be before his own bones were picked clean by the giant bird?

He turned the skull over in his hands and looked into its empty sockets. Suddenly he was furious. He would not let the cruel man destroy him.

He explored every inch of that mountaintop. And when he found the bird's nest, he knew there was hope. He hid under the nest's rim and waited until the giant bird landed. Then he jumped up and grabbed its legs.

The bird let out an ear-splitting squawk. Then it soared into the sky, with Yusef hanging on beneath. It spiraled upward, gliding on the currents of hot air that rose from the sun-baked earth. Yusef's arms began to ache. His fingers cramped, but he held tight, waiting for the bird to dive low. And when it finally did, he closed his eyes and dropped to the ground.

He landed hard, tumbling over rough sand and stones, but he was safe. So he picked himself up and began walking back to the man's house.

His plan was dangerous, but he was too angry to care. When he finally reached the man's door, he knocked and asked for work.

"Of course," said the man. "I can always use another boy."

Just as Yusef had hoped, the man didn't recognize him. The boy's face was bruised and swollen from the fall. Besides, the man would never imagine anyone returning from the mountaintop.

Soon after, the man sent Yusef to kill a bull and skin it, and it wasn't long before they traveled back to the base of the mountain. Again the man ordered the boy to lie down on the hide.

"Show me how," said Yusef.

"What? You want me to ruin my cloak on that bloody hide?" roared the man. He lunged forward, but the boy slipped aside, tripping the man with his foot.

And while the man lay stunned, Yusef whipped the hide around him and tied it tight. Then he hid behind a rock.

Again the giant bird swooped down and grasped the hide, this time with the man inside it. Again it flew to the top of the mountain, and again it was frightened away.

When the man struggled free, he raced to the edge.

"Hurry," Yusef shouted from below, "throw me the gems that are around your feet."

The man recognized his own words. But they were coming from the lips of the boy—the very boy, he now realized, he had left on the mountaintop a few days earlier.

The man bellowed with rage. He kicked the hide over the edge in a shower of gems and tore the bird's nest to shreds. And while Yusef picked up diamonds and rubies, the man heaved bones at the bird circling overhead. It flew away, never to return.

The man ran back to the edge of the mountain and saw the boy riding away with bags full of gems. "Wait!" howled the man. "How did you get down?"

"I flew."

"Flew?" the man screeched, suddenly realizing he should not have chased away the giant bird. "But how will I get down?"

The boy kept riding, but his words floated up to the mountaintop.

"Don't ask me. Ask the bones!"

The Four-Footed Horror

Morning, noon and night, the man kicked at the little black dog.

For some reason, the dog was always dripping wet, even on sunny days. And the man could not stand the smell of its damp fur. He tried to chase the dog out of his cabin. He threw his boots at it and even shot at it, but nothing frightened the little black dog. Finally, he went after it with his broom, but his broom swished right through it.

That's when the man noticed something that chilled him to the bone. The dog cast no shadow. The man shivered, because now he knew—that dog was a *ghost*.

The dog followed him everywhere he went, sometimes making its presence known with a cold draft on the man's ankles. Sometimes it appeared as the tip of one black ear, twitching nearby, or as a pair of disembodied eyes.

And every time that dog came near, the man screamed.

Neighbors heard him for miles around. They watched him running down the road, dodging and hopping, as if something were nipping at his heels. But no one saw a thing.

They began to whisper about him and hurry to the other side of the road when he dashed past.

One evening, the man tried to lure the dog outside his cabin by leaving a bowl of food on the porch, and a bowl of water, too. But that very night, the dog slipped into the man's bed and burrowed under his blankets to warm itself. The man woke up freezing.

And when he saw that ice-cold dog with its head on his pillow, he leaped straight into the air with a bloodcurdling yell.

He hit the floor running, pulled on his trousers, and raced down to the barn. He grabbed his saddlebags, packed one with hay and grain and the other with apples and biscuits. Then he jumped on his mule and galloped right out of Kentucky. The more miles he put between himself and that dog, the better.

When he finally reached Missouri he stopped to spend the night in a deserted cabin. He was sore from the long ride, hungry, and desperately tired.

But when he opened the door, what did he see?

The little black dog.

Well, the man just about jumped out of his skin. He threw himself on his mule and rode all the way back to Kentucky. By now he was about to collapse, and so was the mule. And when he looked into his cabin, he fainted.

There was the little black dog.

When he came to, he saw that the dog was carrying a bone in its mouth, and it certainly wasn't a hog bone. It was a human bone, from a human leg—a dripping wet human bone—and that dog was trying to drop it right on the man's foot.

He leaped to his feet and ran screeching down the road with the dog chasing him, the leg bone clutched in its teeth.

Even the meanest dogs in the county slunk away when they sensed that little black dog coming, their tails tucked between their legs.

But the man couldn't get away from his ghostly companion. All the time he was pounding on his neighbor's door, the dog was trying to drop that bone on him. "Help!" he cried.

The neighbor peered out the window and watched the man hop around the porch, kicking at nothing. The neighbor was afraid to open his door, but he finally came out and asked, "What's wrong?"

"I haven't had a moment's peace," the man cried, "since I killed a bothersome peddler, and his dog too, and threw them both in my pond.

"See that little black dog," he sobbed. "It's come back to haunt me."

The neighbor couldn't see it. But he went to get the sheriff, and they pulled the bones out of the pond. Then they buried the bones of that loyal dog in the graveyard right beside the bones of its master and took the killer off to jail.

And where was the jail? Right beside the graveyard.

The man never saw the little black dog again. But it haunted him for the rest of his life. Whenever he fell asleep at night, he was awakened by the overpowering smell of wet dog.

Beginning with the Ears

There once was a man named Abdu who had trouble finding work. He was very poor, and his wife and children were always hungry.

In desperation, Abdu left the town where he lived to see if he could earn a few coins in the countryside. But no matter how far he walked, he found no one who needed his help. By afternoon, he was weak and tired, for he had not had a bite to eat all day.

Suddenly he saw an old woman coming toward him. She was bent and wrinkled and wore a flowered kerchief over her hair. "Where are you going?" she asked.

"Who knows," he cried. "I must wander from place to place until I earn enough to support my wife and children."

"Do not despair," she said. "Bring your family to live with me, Abdu, and we will share my wealth."

Abdu was amazed. "Who are you?" he asked. "And how do you know my name?"

"I'm your cousin," she replied. "I'm old and alone and would like your company. If you and your family live with me, no one will have to go hungry."

Abdu could hardly believe his ears, and hope began to grow in his heart. He felt strong again, and he ran home to tell his wife and children all that he had heard. They were delighted to learn of their long-lost cousin.

That very evening they left town and walked out to meet the old woman, who was waiting for them in the middle of the road.

She took them home and let them eat to their hearts' content. "And soon you shall have milk to drink," she told them. She picked up a pail and went out to the barn.

Abdu's wife followed to see if she could help with the milking, but as she approached the barn, she overheard the old woman talking to her cow. "Tomorrow I shall eat my guests," she said.

The cow mooed as if to say, "No, no, no!" And Abdu's wife rushed back to the house to warn her husband.

"We must leave at once," she cried. "The old woman told the cow she is planning to eat us tomorrow!"

Abdu was angry. "You didn't hear right," he said. "Look how kind and generous she has been."

Abdu's wife finally agreed to stay, but she was too frightened to sleep all night.

The next morning, Abdu's wife again followed the old woman out to the barn. Again she overheard what the old woman said. "Ah, today I shall eat my guests!" And again the cow mooed as if to say, "No, no, no!"

Abdu's wife ran back to the house as fast as she could. "We can't stay here a moment longer. The old woman is planning to eat us today!" she cried. But still Abdu refused to listen.

"Is there something wrong with your ears?" she shouted. "Stay if you like, but I am taking the children back home." And that is exactly what she did.

When the old woman returned from the barn and saw that only Abdu was left, she decided to eat him right away. She blocked the doorway and screeched at him, "I'm not your cousin!" Her back straightened, her wrinkles faded away, and her kerchief fell off, revealing long, dark hair. "I am a witch," she said, "who likes nothing better than eating the fools who come to live in my house!

"Tell me," she asked, "which part of your body should I eat first?" She pulled a metal file from her pocket and began to sharpen her teeth.

Abdu was trembling from head to toe. He realized he was trapped and there was nothing he could do.

"My wife warned me," he said, "but I would not listen. So begin with my ears."

Fiddling with Fire

Never before had Lucas visited the cemetery at night. Never had he been there alone. A chill wind was blowing through the trees, sending moon shadows slithering across the gravestones.

Lucas shivered, but he knew he must stay. That's what he'd been told by an old granny woman: "If you want to learn to fiddle, go to the graveyard alone and practice all night.

"But don't be greedy," she'd whispered, and Lucas had seen fear in her eyes.

He wanted to run home, but he forced himself to sit on a mossy gravestone and tuck his fiddle under his chin. He drew the bow across the strings. The screeching and squawking were unbearable. He stopped for a moment and heard a chorus of frogs croaking in the nearby meadow. "They sound better than I do," he moaned.

But he took up his fiddle and tried again. This time he hit a few melodious notes. Lucas was so excited that he didn't notice a whiff of smoke in the air.

He practiced hour after hour. The smoke grew thicker, but Lucas noticed nothing but his music. The screeching and squawking were gone now. Still he wasn't satisfied.

"I wish I were the best fiddler in the world," he shouted to the moon.

"You can be," said a voice from behind his back.

Lucas whirled around, his heart in his throat.

There stood a horrifying figure, dressed in a long black cloak lined with red and smoldering at the hem. His black boots were licked by tongues of flame. And his pointed tail thrashed smoke from side to side. Lucas cringed, for now he knew who'd been teaching him to fiddle that night.

"Give it here," demanded the devil. And he began to play. His fingers danced over the strings and firmly guided the bow. Songs burst forth, so bewitching that Lucas could think of nothing else. "I didn't know you could play," gasped Lucas.

"Play?" snapped the devil. "I invented the fiddle." And he began a fiery tune. His fingers moved in a blur.

"I'd give anything to play like that," Lucas cried.

An evil grin spread across the devil's face. "Even your soul?"

Lucas felt the hot breath of the devil upon him. He drew back, shuddering. But then the devil resumed playing. "You can keep your soul until you die," said the devil, "then it's mine." He played so passionately that Lucas began to clap his hands and stomp his feet.

"Where can you find a better deal?" asked the devil.

So Lucas agreed to sell his soul, his fears swept aside by the devil's music.

But he could hardly stand doing what the devil demanded next.

"To seal our pact, you must swallow my spit!"

"I can't," said Lucas.

"You don't want to be the world's best fiddler?"

"I do," said Lucas, and he squeezed his eyes shut and swallowed. The devil's spit was hot and sulfurous. Lucas could feel it burning all the way down to his stomach. He thought he was going to be sick. But then the devil handed Lucas his fiddle, and all seemed well.

A flaming hole opened in the ground, and the gleeful prince of darkness sank from sight, sucking the smoke down with him.

Lucas fiddled and danced all the way home.

From that night on, no one could get enough of Lucas's fiddling. He made that fiddle laugh and sing. And when he played for parties, everyone danced until cock's crow. He played up river and down, over the hills and through the valleys. He never tired of playing.

When Lucas was young, his fiddle sang with joy, but as he grew older, sadness crept in. The thought of spending eternity in the devil's fiery realm preyed upon his mind. So Lucas began to scheme. He had to think of a way to outwit the devil.

One moonlit night, Lucas had an idea. He jumped out of bed and raced to the cemetery. The slithering shadows made Lucas wonder if spirits had slipped from their graves. He shuddered, but he sat on the mossy tombstone once more and tucked his fiddle beneath his chin. Then he dragged his bow across the strings, making them screech as they did so long ago.

Just when Lucas thought he couldn't stand his awful fiddling a moment longer, a fiery hole opened up. And once again the prince of darkness stood before him. Lucas leaped to his feet, trembling, but he continued to play.

"Stop that squawking!" bellowed the devil. "You are hurting my ears."

"I can't," said Lucas. "This is the best I can do."

The devil snorted fire and stamped his cloven hooves right through the charred soles of his boots.

"I'm no longer the best fiddler in the world," Lucas said, trying to keep his voice from quivering.

"You are!" bellowed the devil. "Try harder!" And he

threw thunderbolts so close to Lucas's head that they curled his hair.

Lucas jumped back, but he made his fiddle screech even worse than before. Gooseflesh crept up his neck, making his hair stand on end. But he looked the devil in the eye. "Our pact is broken."

"It is *not!*" screamed the devil, holding his hands over his ears.

"It *is*," said Lucas, scraping his bow across the strings once more.

"All *right!*" the devil snarled. "You can keep your soul on one condition. You must *never* play the fiddle again."

Then he sank through a circle of flames and the fiery hole closed behind him.

"Never play the fiddle again?" Lucas trudged home, sobbing. He put his fiddle in a trunk and closed the lid.

Then he took to his bed, feeling old and weary. He shriveled a little each day and spoke to no one. But when his family gathered around, he made a last request. "I want to hold my fiddle one more time."

He ran his fingers over the smooth wood and quietly fingered the strings. Then, in a rush of unexpected strength, he played a haunting melody.

"Now put it away," he said. And they did.

But before he could sink back on his pillow, terror overtook him. He tried to shield his eyes from something no one else could see. A bolt of lightning hit. It blinded everyone around him. When they recovered their sight, they couldn't see anything on the bed except scorched sheets.

And when they looked for the fiddle, they saw a smoking hole in the lid of the trunk—and nothing inside.

The Laplander's Drum

Will couldn't take his eyes off the mysterious drum. Its wooden bowl was covered with tightly stretched reindeer hide, and on that hide were the eeriest drawings Will had ever seen. From the drum's edge, three brass rings dangled on leather thongs.

"Who wants me to tell his fortune?" cried the Lappish drummer. His eyes were pale as arctic ice, and when he faced the English crowd, he seemed to be staring at other worlds far beyond.

The townspeople murmured to one another, curious but wary. No one stepped forward.

But Will felt himself irresistibly drawn to the drummer's side. "I do," the boy said. "I want to know my fortune."

53

He handed a coin to the drummer and watched him lift the dangling brass rings and place them on the drumhead.

Then the drumming began. The Laplander beat his drum with the horns of a reindeer, slowly, softly, not disturbing the rings at all. But as the pace quickened, the ornately carved rings began to bounce over the drawings. They encircled great round eyes, suns and moons, fish with two heads, four-legged birds, animals and monsters of every shape and size. The rings bounced across letters of an ancient alphabet, and signs and symbols known only to wizards.

When the drummer stopped, he looked at the rings. A demonic grin lit up his face. One ring had landed between drawings, encircling nothing. The second encircled a monkey and the third encircled the chain that led to the monkey's collar.

Will was merely curious until he glanced at the drummer's face. Then he felt a twinge of fear. What *was* his fortune? What gave the drummer such fiendish glee?

Will stepped back, nervously waiting for the drummer to speak, and then he heard his father's voice echoing across the town square. "You!" he shouted. "You with the drum! I'm the magistrate. Show me your pass."

The drummer pulled forth a crumpled piece of paper, but the magistrate refused to accept it, insisting it was a forgery. "Lock him up," he told the constable. "I'll keep his drum."

But before the drummer was led away, he issued a challenge to Will. "I dare you," he said, "to use my drum."

"Never!" said Will's father. "*No one* will touch it."

The drummer crowed with laughter as he walked to the jail.

That night Will lay awake, too uneasy to sleep. He heard branches sighing in the breeze, revelers walking home from the inn.

And drumming?

Was it possible?

He lay absolutely still, listening. It started as soft tapping on the doors of the magistrate's house, then moved to the walls, then to the roof, repeating the circuit, louder each time. Stranger yet, no dog in the household barked.

Will heard his father rouse the servants to search for an intruder. But no one was there. And the servants said they heard nothing.

But father and son heard the drumming for weeks, as if the drummer were trying to enter their home, trying to find his drum. Yet all the while, the drummer sat in the jail across the square.

Will could hardly stand the drumming. Night and day, it reminded him of his mysterious fortune, the one the brass rings had foretold.

He wanted to question the drummer, but his father forbade it. "Stay away from that man," he said.

So Will spent hours in his room, his mind racing. He *had* to learn more about his fortune, the only way he could, by examining the forbidden drum.

The very first evening his father was away, he slipped into his office to search for it. He looked in every cabinet, every drawer. He looked behind draperies. He pulled books from the shelves. But he had no luck until he remembered the window seat with the storage space beneath. He lifted the seat.

And there it was. The drum with all its eerie drawings. The drum with the picture of a chained monkey.

Will knew his father would be furious if he touched it. But he wanted to look at it more closely. Just look, that was all. So he carried it up to his room. It was as cold to the touch as an arctic night.

Will stared at the drawing of the chained monkey and was startled to see that its hands were now raised to its cheeks, and its mouth was wide open as if it were screaming.

And somehow, the monkey's face was looking more like the face of a boy.

Will felt like throwing the drum out the window, yet his hands clutched it more tightly. And while he held it, it grew warm.

It began to pulsate faintly beneath his fingers.

It seemed alive.

To Will's horror, his hands picked up the brass rings, set

them upon the drum, grasped the reindeer horns and began to play.

Even more alarming, he heard echoing drumbeats from across the square—and he felt a surge of power down to his fingertips.

No matter how hard he tried to still his hands, they beat the drum faster. The echoes quickened and the brass rings bounced.

Will thought maybe he could break free from the drum if he returned it to his father's office. But his legs would not obey him. Panic swept over him, but there was nothing he could do.

His hands drummed faster. The echoes grew louder. The brass rings bounced higher and higher until they bounced right off the edge of the drum.

While the rings were dangling from their leather thongs, suspended in space, a fierce drumbeat echoed across the square and in through the open window.

Will's entire room vanished—he could see nothing.

When his father returned home and found that the drum was not in the office, he raced to Will's bedroom. But he could not find the door.

He ran outside to get a ladder so he could climb through Will's window. But all he could see was a blank wall.

"This is the drummer's doing," cried Will's father. And he ran across the town square to the jail.

The drummer looked at the magistrate coldly. "You

want me to help you?" he asked. "How can I? Your boy has my drum."

"I'll give back your drum when we find it. I'll give back your freedom. I'll sign your pass, provide you with a horse, and give you fine new clothes."

A bitter smile flickered across the drummer's face, but he followed the magistrate to his home. They climbed the stairs and hurried down the hall to the spot where the magistrate had last seen Will's door.

The moment they arrived, the drummer bared his chest. He began to drum upon it with a primitive, powerful beat.

From somewhere in the void, the magic drum began to reverberate faintly. The drummer beat his chest harder, his fists tightly clenched, his eyes flashing. The echoing drumbeats grew louder.

Finally the magistrate saw the room materialize—and Will, too, still holding the drum. The father rushed in and knocked the drum from his son's grasp, releasing him from its spell.

He knew he'd promised to give it back, but when the drummer picked it up, the magistrate turned on him. "I refuse to help you," he shouted. "You're a wizard. You should be burned at the stake."

The drummer's only reply came in a few swift drumbeats. When the brass rings landed on drawings of monsters, the drummer struck the drumhead fiercely, one more time. Father and son watched in horror as the drawings rose up through the rings and grew, turning into flesh and blood, fur and fangs, snarling about the room.

The last that anyone saw of the magistrate, he was racing down the road as if monsters were pursuing him.

The drummer turned his icy eyes on Will. "Your fate," he said, "is with me." He pulled a chain and a monkey collar from under his cloak and reached out for the boy.

A Night of Terror

One evening two rabbinical students were hurrying down a forest path. They had planned to spend the night in the next village, but now dark clouds were rolling in, and lightning split the sky.

Thunder blasted them from every side. They cupped their hands over their ears, but they couldn't protect themselves from the rain. It poured off their hats and drenched their clothing. They ran through the dark forest, splashing and stumbling, hoping to find shelter.

Finally they spotted a dim light ahead, and they raced along the path to a small cottage. Its door was ajar, and when the students knocked, two monstrous dogs burst out. They growled and snarled and barked so ferociously that the students backed away.

All at once two sisters appeared in the cottage doorway. "Don't worry," they said. "The dogs are just defending us." The women snapped their fingers, and the dogs crept back into the cottage.

The students were amazed. But they thought the sisters looked kindly and pious, so they asked if they could spend the night.

"And won't you have a bite to eat with us?" the sisters asked.

Now the students were very hungry, but before they sat down at the table, they noticed one sister stirring the kettle of boiling broth with her bare fingers and saw the other taking hot bread from the oven with her bare hands. The young men trembled, because they knew they were watching witches prepare enchanted food.

The two students stared at each other. The storm was still raging. Lightning struck a tree outside with a thunderous blast. But what could be more dangerous than staying *inside* with a pair of *witches*?

"We are not hungry after all," said one student, trying to keep his voice steady.

"And we really should be on our way," said the other, edging toward the door.

"Nonsense," said one witch.

The other witch snapped her fingers, and the dogs trotted over to the door and blocked it. "We really want you to stay," she said. "Besides, the storm is worse."

A Night of Terror

She slashed her hand through the air and lightning bolts encircled the cottage. She clapped, and thunder exploded throughout the forest, shaking the very floor on which they stood.

The students were horrified by the witches' power. They thought silently for a moment. Then one glanced toward the window, and the other nodded—the moment the witches and dogs fell asleep, they would unlatch the window and jump to freedom.

The students said good night and climbed up the ladder to the loft. Their clothes were cold and damp, so they burrowed into the straw bedding. But they didn't sleep.

Every few minutes, they looked over the edge of the loft to see what the witches were doing below. And every time they looked, the witches were wide awake. The women sat in front of the fire, cackling over ancient books filled with ghastly magic spells and potions.

The students burrowed deeper into the straw and waited. At last all was silent. They were getting ready to take one last look, then slip down the ladder, when all of a sudden they heard its bottom rung creak.

One of the witches was on her way up.

Both students pretended to be sleeping. They closed their eyes, but when long, moldy hair brushed their cheeks, they knew a witch was leaning over them.

The students lay absolutely still, but they clenched their fists under the straw. They were ready to lunge at the witch if she tried to put a spell on them. Luckily she just backed down, rung by rung, and whispered to the other witch, "They're asleep." Then the witches rushed to the door and opened it.

"Fetch," they said, and they sent their monstrous dogs down to the barn. Moments later the students heard the sound of hooves, then the lowing of oxen *inside* the cottage. They peered down from the loft.

The witches were slipping halters off four oxen, and the students were shocked to see the oxen turn into four men.

With the hideous dogs snarling at their heels, the four men did everything the witches asked of them. They carried in pails of water from the witches' well. They milked the cows and split wood for the witches' fire.

Then the four men were fed broth and bread, and with the very first bite, they began to turn back into oxen. By the time they had finished eating, they were swishing their tails, walking on all fours, and meekly letting the witches put halters on them once again. Then the dogs herded them back to the barn.

The students were aghast. They thanked God that they hadn't eaten the witches' food themselves, and they slipped back under the straw.

By now the students were desperate, but those witches never did sleep that night. And when the students arose the next morning, the witches already had hot bread and broth on the table.

"You must eat before you go," said one witch.

Both students felt their skin crawl.

"We can't," said one. "We are meeting someone in the next village."

"We are already late," said the other, swallowing hard.

Those witches wanted another pair of oxen, so they tore off chunks of bread and stalked across the room. They faced the students, eye to eye, ready to force the bread into their mouths.

"Perhaps we could take the bread with us," said one student, backing away, "and eat as we walk along."

The witches exchanged glances. "Very well," they said, and they snapped their fingers. The dogs got up and followed the students, just inches from their heels.

"Thank you for the bread," the students called back, running for their lives, with those ferocious dogs racing along behind them.

At first the dogs were just panting, but soon they were growling, then snarling, then snapping their teeth.

And no matter how fast the students went, the dogs kept up with them.

"What about the witches' bread?" cried one student.

"Of course!" cried the other.

They threw the bread to the dogs, expecting them to wolf it down and turn into gentle oxen, but they didn't. The dogs just caught the bread in their great jaws and raced back to the cottage.

A Night of Terror

The students heard hysterical barking echo through the forest, then hideous screams, then silence, broken only by the lowing of oxen.

Did the witches whip the dogs for letting the students escape? Did the dogs kill the witches? And what about the oxen? The students shuddered. They could hardly stand the thought of returning to the cottage. But if the witches were dead, the poor oxen—poor men, really—might starve.

No sooner had the students turned back, than what did they see? The four oxen were lumbering down the path. Somehow they had escaped!

The students rejoiced. They patted the oxen's heads.

"What if *we* took off their halters?" one student asked. "Could we turn them back into men?"

"It's worth a try," said the other. So each grabbed two halters and tugged.

The shaggy fur of the oxen melted away, their horns disappeared and their soft brown eyes turned . . . hard and cold.

For there, in front of the students, stood two monstrous dogs and two grim witches.

The dogs circled the students, snarling.

And the witches advanced on the young men, one with boiling broth, the other with steaming bread.

Nowhere to Hide

Whenever Ivan scooped turnips from an iron pot, he wished for elegant food on a silver platter, food fit for a prince. That's what Ivan wanted to be, a prince, even if it meant marrying the most evil princess in the world.

This princess lived high on a mountaintop, in a castle surrounded by forests that sloped down to the sea. Her father had promised half his kingdom to any suitor who could win her hand.

But the princess didn't wish to marry. So she gave her suitors three chances to hide from her, knowing they could never hide from her magic spyglass.

And when they failed her test—what did she do? She chopped off their heads.

But Ivan wasn't discouraged. He didn't think she would chop off *his* head.

So he packed his knapsack and set forth. On his way to the castle he strode along the beach, dreaming of riches. But soon he was hungry.

He threw a hook into the sea and caught a shiny fish. Just as he was about to toss it in his frying pan, the fish spoke to him. "Spare me!" it gasped, "and someday I will help you. Take one of my silver scales. Burn it when you need me and I will swim to shore."

How could a fish help him? Ivan couldn't imagine. But he took pity on it, plucked one of its scales and tossed the fish back into the sea.

The moment he touched that shimmering scale, he felt a strange tingling at the back of his neck, as if someone were watching him.

He spun around. No one was there. But just as he turned back to the sea, he glimpsed an eye in an incoming wave. A cold, cruel eye that disappeared when the wave broke in a cascade of foam.

Ivan was not easily frightened, but what was that eye? He raced along the sand, his heart pounding. And he didn't stop to rest until the castle path veered from the beach and plunged into the forest.

Ivan leaned against a tree, catching his breath. And while he stood there, he saw an eagle land at the edge of a stream.

He quietly pulled a net from his knapsack, for he was still hungry, and threw it over the eagle.

But the eagle behaved just as oddly as the fish. It begged for its life, offering Ivan a feather which he could burn if he needed the eagle. So Ivan released the great bird.

Needed an eagle?

Ivan would have laughed out loud if he weren't so uneasy. He felt that eerie tingling again, raising the hairs on the back of his neck.

Again he spun around, searching for whoever was watching him. Again he saw no one.

But when he dipped a cupful of water from the stream and lifted it to his lips, he saw that awful eye staring at him intently from the bottom of the cup.

Ivan threw it on the ground and kicked it. He hid behind a tree. When he finally dared to retrieve his cup, the horrible eye had disappeared.

Ivan no longer walked on the trail that was winding its way up to the castle. He stayed off to one side, darting from tree to tree, hoping to hide from the eye that seemed to be following him wherever he went.

But he was getting hungrier by the moment. And when he saw a fox crossing a clearing, he pulled forth his bow and arrow.

"Don't shoot," cried the fox. "Someday you will need me. If you burn a tuft of hair from my chin, I will come."

Ivan hardly dared touch that tuft of hair. He knew what

68

had happened when he touched the fish scale and the feather, but how could he refuse help? He had never been on such a strange journey, and he had no idea what he might encounter next.

So he plucked a tuft of hair from the fox's chin. And even before his neck started tingling, he saw the cruel eye reflected in the shining eye of the fox.

But when he looked over his shoulder, he caught only a glimpse of that eye before it vanished.

Ivan was about to run home, but how could he? He was a brave hunter, a future prince. He would follow that trail all the way to the castle, marry the princess, and live in luxury for the rest of his life.

When he finally reached the palace, he was led inside to meet the princess. "You're a fool to think you can hide from me," she said, "but you may try. I will look for you in the morning."

The hunter stared at her. Somehow she looked familiar. "Stop staring," she said, stamping her foot. And she ordered him out of the throne room.

The hunter raced far from the palace and burned the eagle's feather. "Hide me!" he shouted. Moments later the eagle grasped the hunter with its mighty talons and flew to a distant mountain that pierced the sky. There it dropped the hunter into its nest and covered him with its wings.

In the morning the princess pulled out her magic spyglass. It sent her eye wherever she looked. She could see everything on the earth, under the water and up in the sky. She could see her suitors, wherever they hid.

She pointed her spyglass out the window and looked for the hunter. Her eye roamed over the earth and under the water. It didn't see him. But when it traveled across the sky, it noticed two hairs of the hunter's fur hat peeking out from under the eagle's wings.

When the hunter returned to the palace, he was already dreaming of meat pies and purple robes.

But the princess mocked him. "I saw you in the eagle's nest," she said. "You have only two more chances to hide."

The hunter was shocked. He'd heard rumors about her spyglass, but he had no idea it was so powerful. He hurried to the sea and burned the fish's silver scale. "Come help me!" he cried.

The fish immediately swam to shore, along with a huge shark. It told the shark to swallow the hunter whole and swim to the very depths of the ocean. But later the shark opened its mouth to eat a smaller fish—at the very moment the magic spyglass sent the princess's eye beneath the waves. And there, between the shark's pointed teeth, it glimpsed one thread of the hunter's coat.

The hunter was sure no one could have seen him hidden in a shark's belly at the bottom of the sea, but when he entered the throne room, the princess laughed at him. "I saw you inside the shark," she said. "If you can't find a better

hiding place tonight, your head will roll across the court-yard tomorrow."

The hunter was beginning to fear that she might be right. Now he realized with horror where he'd seen her cruel eyes—in the wave at the beach and in the cup in the forest. But he rushed outside, determined to try again. He burned the fox's hair and called for help.

The fox bounded to his side. "Fear not," it said, and it led him into a tunnel it had dug under the palace. The hunter crawled after the fox until they reached a spot di-rectly under the princess's room. They could hear her foot-steps overhead. When morning came they heard her walk over to the window. At first all was silent. Then she began talking to herself. "Not in the sky," she said. And a little later, "Not in the ocean." Later yet she shouted, *"Not on the earth?"* That's when she threw her spyglass against the wall and smashed it into a thousand pieces.

"I'm safe," cried the hunter.

He was thanking the fox for saving him when he heard the angry princess stamping her foot on the floor above his head. *Crack!* Her leg came down through a rotten board over the tunnel. She pulled her leg out and peered through the jagged hole with those cold, cruel eyes.

"I found you!" she said.

The Handkerchief

Long ago in China there lived an old man with a heart of stone. He drove away every beggar who came to his door.

The old man and his wife lived by themselves, for they had no children. Nor did they have servants, because the old man hated to pay anyone.

In time, his wife grew so feeble she had to have help. At first the old man was angry. "Why can't you do what you have always done?" he grumbled. But his wife couldn't manage, no matter how hard she tried. Finally the old man decided he would never get his meals on time unless he hired a servant girl, so at last he did.

The girl tried her best to serve her master faithfully, but she soon found that nothing she did pleased the old man.

The Handkerchief

The crack of his whip was heard throughout the house, and night after night he beat the girl so badly that she fell asleep crying. The old man's wife heard the pitiful cries, but she said nothing and did nothing, for she was afraid of her husband.

All of the old man's neighbors called him "Cruel One," and even the saints and gods heard of his evil ways. They wanted to test him, so one of the gods turned himself into a barefooted beggar and went to the old man's door.

"Master of the house!" he called out. "Please bring me something to eat. I am starving."

It happened that only the servant girl was home that morning. She felt sorry for the miserable beggar, and she gave him a bag of rice that she had gleaned for herself from the rice straw that she burned in the stove.

"Take this rice," she said, "but hurry away before my master comes back. There will be trouble if he sees you here. He is evil."

The beggar took the bag of rice and thanked the girl for her kindness. In return, he gave her a handkerchief. It looked like a humble gift, but a god in disguise can give a present that is far more remarkable than it seems. "Wash your face with this magic cloth every day," he told her, "but be sure no one else ever uses it."

The girl slipped it under her sash, just in time, as the old man and his wife returned. Her master was so furious to

74

find a beggar at their door that he chased him away with a stick. Then he beat the servant girl for not driving the beggar away.

The girl fled to her room to wash away her tears with the magic handkerchief. Not only did the pain mysteriously vanish, but she grew more beautiful.

The old man wondered why the servant girl looked prettier each day despite the beatings. "Tell me your secret," he demanded.

But the girl didn't want to tell him about the handkerchief, for she knew he would beat her even harder if he learned about the rice she had given to the beggar. And what if he took the handkerchief away?

The girl endured her beatings silently, but one day she forgot and pulled forth the soothing handkerchief while her master's eyes were still upon her. He tore it out of her hands and insisted that she tell him everything. And when he learned that the beggar had given her the handkerchief after she had given him rice, the old man said the handkerchief belonged to him. "Everything in this house belongs to me, including the rice you gave away and the handkerchief you got in return."

"But the beggar said no one else should use it," the servant girl cried. He paid no attention.

When the girl wept that night, she had nothing to wash away her tears and pain. Nor could she sleep, for she had

failed to keep her handkerchief safe. What if her master used it? Would her luck turn even worse?

The next morning the old man hurried to the washbasin so he could use the handkerchief himself. He wanted his looks to improve as much as the servant girl's, so he washed his face repeatedly. But each time he lowered the magic handkerchief, his wife's eyes opened wider. He thought she was impressed to see him become so handsome.

In truth, her eyes were wide with horror, for she saw what the magic handkerchief had done. But as always, she said nothing.

The old man handed the handkerchief to her. "I want a beautiful wife," he said. "Use it."

She held it between two fingertips as if it might bite her.

"What are you waiting for?" he shouted, picking up the whip he used on the servant girl.

His wife, who had never disobeyed him before, dropped the handkerchief and hurried out of the room. He could not understand her odd behavior. But when he stooped to pick up that handkerchief, he saw before him a clawed and hairy hand.

He rushed to the mirror. Staring back at him was a strange beast with bloodshot eyes, sharp fangs, and matted hair.

The Mousetrap

The wizard leaned into the wind, cursing the storm. The gale was so fierce it endangered ships along the rocky coast. But the wizard thought only of the salt spray whipping his face and the icy rain dripping down his neck.

He usually stayed close to his hearth when such vile weather battered Iceland. But today his favorite dinner was being served at the inn—boiled sheeps' heads and pickled blood loaf. How could he possibly stay home when such delicacies awaited him?

When he arrived, he shook the rainwater from his shoulders and sat down at a table by the window. An unpleasant neighbor was sitting across the room, so the wizard mumbled a few magical words. Then he watched as the neighbor swigged down a mouthful of milk—and turned ashen.

The Mousetrap

The milk that was fine just moments before had suddenly become sickeningly sour.

The wizard smirked, but for only a moment, before he became gloomy again. He was a failure, capable of only the simplest tricks. He could turn milk sour or send those who annoyed him into sneezing fits.

But somehow the immense powers of his father, his grandfather, and his great-grandfather had eluded him.

He slowly chewed the last bite of pickled blood loaf and looked out the window at the raging waters beyond the harbor. He saw a small ship there, rising and falling with the waves. Its icy decks were awash, its mast broken in two. And as he watched, he saw a wall of water crash down upon the ship and thrust it from sight.

He saw sailors bobbing to the surface, clinging to bits of wreckage, and he watched his fellow villagers brave the storm to rescue them.

All the while, the wizard sat by the window, unconcerned. It wasn't until the survivors were huddled around the inn fire, bemoaning the loss of their precious cargo, that the wizard's interest was kindled.

"Our bags of coins are spilled all over the ocean floor," cried one sailor. "We can never reclaim them."

The story of sunken treasure jolted the wizard's memory. He jumped up, wrapped himself in his cloak, and raced up the hillside to his home.

The wizard's house was built like all the others in the

village, of stone and timber, faced with sod. But no one had a hearthstone quite like his.

The wizard knelt before the fire, pressed the back corner of the hearthstone, and watched it swing upward on sturdy hinges, exposing a secret hiding place beneath. And in that secret place was a book, its leather cover falling apart, its pages tattered. But this precious book, handed down for generations, contained the very passage the wizard needed.

He paged through it until he found the words he dimly remembered—a spell for redeeming treasure from the depths of the sea.

He began reading aloud:

First weave a net using hair from a maiden. Then place that net on the surface of the ocean, above the spot where the treasure has sunk. The net will catch a tide mouse. Once it's caught, put the mouse in a barrel, offer it wheat and water, and give it a bed of maiden's hair.

Then steal a coin and slip it under the mouse's bedding. If all is done correctly, the tide mouse will draw coins out of the sea each day.

The wizard's eyes were aglow until he read the warning:

Any man who keeps such a mouse places himself in great danger, for he must not possess the mouse when he dies. If he

The Mousetrap

fails to give it away in time, violent mouse squalls will roar across the ocean, tearing up the land, and the man will die in agony. But when he gives the mouse away, he must warn the new owner of its danger or the very earth will smite him.

Surely, thought the wizard, he wasn't about to die. So he memorized the words he'd read, replaced the book in the hole beneath the hearthstone, and pressed the stone back into place. He was going to do exactly what the book said, with no mistakes.

The next morning he followed a young shepherdess up the slope of a slumbering volcano that towered above the town. The mountain had not spit forth ash and fire since the wizard was a child.

While the sheep nibbled on scarce bits of moss and grass between the rocks, the girl napped. And while she napped, the wizard quietly snipped off her golden braids, without a thought about how she would feel when she discovered her loss.

He rushed home with the maiden's hair, but his book gave him no magic formula for making a net. So he struggled to tie the hair into knots, forming a mesh with openings so small that no mouse could slip through.

When the winds died down, he rowed out to the spot where the ship's treasure had sunk. He dropped the net of maiden's hair on the water and watched over it from sunrise until sunset. Finally, just before dark, he saw a mouse's paw entangled in the net. In one quick motion, he scooped it out of the water and into his pocket. Then he buttoned up his pocket and rowed home.

He had the barrel ready for the tide mouse, with the wheat and water and a bed of maiden's hair. But he had not yet stolen a coin.

So the next morning he waited until his neighbor went fishing. Then he sneaked into his house, snatched a coin, and raced home to tuck it under the mouse's bed.

All that night he sat beside the barrel brooding. Would the coins pour in? Or would his magic fail as it had so often in the past? He checked again and again, growing irritable. Even angry. But just before sunrise the mouse's bed rose, pushed up by a stack of coins.

"At last!" the wizard cried. He rejoiced that morning and each morning thereafter when he scooped up the coins.

He now had so much money that he often treated himself to boiled sheeps' heads and pickled blood loaf. And still the coins piled up.

Having such wealth pleased the wizard. But more than anything, he relished his newfound power. He had mastered the magic of his ancestors. How proud they would have been.

Year after year, the coins came, and year after year the wizard grew older. He knew he didn't need so much money, but how could he give up his magic mouse?

The Mousetrap

It wasn't until he grew quite feeble that fear began to overwhelm him. What if he still had the mouse in his possession when he died?

Every storm rolling across the sea began to look like a mouse squall headed his way, ready to destroy the land and send him to an agonizing death. But each time, he gritted his teeth and told himself, "Tomorrow. I will give the mouse away tomorrow."

Then one morning the wizard felt sharp pains in his chest, and he could no longer contain his terror. When he looked far across the ocean, he saw huge thunderheads above the waves, lightning ripping across the sky, and sheets of water pouring down.

He must give away the mouse. He slipped it into his pocket and headed down to the harbor. The only man he found there was a fisherman repairing his nets. The man laughed when the wizard described what the mouse could do.

All the while the storm was coming closer.

Finally the wizard pulled forth coins that the mouse had drawn from the sea—coins that looked as if they had lain on the ocean floor ever since the shipwreck.

He knew he should tell the fisherman about the danger of keeping the mouse too long. But there was no time.

The mouse squall was almost upon them.

"Look," he said. His hands trembled as he held out the coins.

"Well," said the fisherman at last. "I'll give it a try." And he accepted the mouse, tucking it into his own pocket before he walked away.

The wizard could still feel his heart pounding in his throat. But now he saw the storm veering away to the north. He heard a tremendous boom but thought nothing of it, for he had just saved himself from an agonizing death. He took a deep breath, only to cough violently. For suddenly the air was thick with volcanic dust and sulfurous fumes.

He heard a crackling roar and turned in time to see a stream of boiling lava pour down the side of the old volcano. It had already swallowed his home, his book of magic, his coins, and all.

Now it was going to swallow him.

The Speaking Head

The boy felt uneasy, traveling to a distant land with a merchant he barely knew. He was going to meet the man's daughter, his future bride. But he had never left Prague before, nor had he been separated from his family.

Joseph was only twelve when the merchant approached his father to arrange for the betrothal. It seemed as if the two rich men had made a fine match for their children. But when the merchant wanted Joseph to visit his castle, the father hesitated. The boy's Bar Mitzvah was only six months away, and the trip to the castle would take weeks.

But Joseph was an exceptional student. The merchant promised not only to help the boy with his studies but also to bring him home long before his Bar Mitzvah. So the boy's parents reluctantly agreed to let him go, and Joseph set forth to meet his future bride.

He could not believe his eyes when he and the merchant finally reached the castle, high on a hill. It was immense, with hundreds of rooms and a great tower that brushed the sky.

When they opened the massive front door, the merchant called for his servants. But no one answered. He called to his wife and daughter. But no one came. "They must be visiting elsewhere this week," he said, as if he weren't the least bit surprised.

Yet it seemed strange to Joseph. And when three full months had passed with no sign of the merchant's family, he became anxious. Besides, the merchant had not given him any help with his studies. Indeed, Joseph had not seen a single book anywhere in the castle.

Joseph passed the time wandering up and down the corridors. He discovered that doors were open to every room except one. And the one locked room was at the very top of the castle tower.

Finally he asked the merchant if he could see what was in that room. "Of course," said the merchant, and they climbed up the tower stairs.

When the merchant unlocked the door, he led the boy inside. Joseph was delighted to see that they had entered a library filled with books. "You will find everything you need for your studies here," the merchant said.

But while Joseph hurried over to the bookcase, the merchant slipped out the door—and turned the key.

Joseph was trapped.

He ran to the door and tried to open it. He tugged at the handle only to find that it was firmly locked from the outside.

He pounded on the door with his fists and called to the merchant. But the only response was the sound of footsteps descending the stairs—until an eerie voice spoke from somewhere in the very same room.

"I see they have found a new victim," it said.

The boy wheeled around and saw a sight so shocking that he almost fainted, for across the library, sitting on a round table, was an old man's head, severed from his body. And that head was speaking to him.

"Who . . . who are you?" cried Joseph.

"Eighty years ago I was a young boy like you," it said, "when I, too, was trapped in this room by the evil demon who pretends he is a merchant."

Joseph shuddered. "But what happened?"

"On the day of my Bar Mitzvah, the merchant came to me with his fellow demons. First they cut off my head. Then they wrote a spell on parchment and placed it under my tongue.

"That spell reveals all secrets to me and forces me to reveal those secrets to them. But a speaking head is good for only eighty years, and now they need a new one."

Joseph felt as if the ground had split open beneath his feet. "The merchant wants my head," he moaned. "That's why he brought me to this terrible place."

"But it's not too late for you to escape," whispered the head. "Listen carefully."

Joseph forced himself to move closer so he could hear, even though the sight of that severed head made him feel faint.

"Your only hope," it whispered, "is to escape through the secret passage. See the bookcase behind you? Push hard on the third shelf."

Joseph pushed and was amazed to see it swing open, revealing a dark passage. He was about to rush in when the speaking head called him back.

"Wait! If you don't take me with you, I'll be forced to reveal how you escaped and where you can be found. But if you do take me, I can guide you."

Joseph went back to the table and gingerly lifted that gruesome head. He put it under his arm, entered the dark passage, and pulled the bookcase shut behind him. Joseph stood trembling in the dark. How could he move ahead with no torch?

"Count seven hundred and three stairs," the head told him. "Then feel for a door."

The Speaking Head

Joseph knew he had not climbed that many steps on his way up to the tower room. Was the speaking head in league with the demons? Did he dare let it guide him?

He felt rooted to the floor until he heard terrible voices crying out, searching for him. He frantically felt for the edge of the step with his foot and moved into the darkness, forever downward.

His fingers ached from clutching the speaking head. The only thing worse than carrying it would be dropping it and letting it roll down the steps, leaving him alone in that terrible place.

He continued down, trying to shut out the demons' voices, trying to remember to count. When he reached the seven hundred and third step, he was breathing hard, and his legs were quivering. He felt for a door—and found it.

But what was on the other side? He was almost afraid to turn the knob. Then he heard a demonic voice so close behind him that it made his ears ache. He thrust open the door, leaped out, and slammed it shut. Before him was a sunlit meadow, far below the castle.

For the first time in eighty years, the speaking head smiled.

Joseph was so relieved he laughed out loud. "Can you guide me home?" he asked.

"Of course," said the speaking head.

And so it was that Joseph finally made his way back to Prague with the aid of the speaking head. He arrived on

the day of his Bar Mitzvah and entered the synagogue with the speaking head under his arm.

All who had gathered there to pray for him listened to his terrible tale with amazement.

Then the speaking head made a last request.

"Remove from my mouth the parchment on which the spell is written, so I can go peacefully to my grave."

When the parchment was removed, the speaking head died. He was given an honorable funeral, attended by all the Jews of Prague.

Joseph slowly recovered from his ordeal. But for many years he was haunted by terrible nightmares in which he was nothing more than a head resting on a table, with no body. And he always woke up screaming.

• A Tale from the United States •

The Dripping Cutlass

There was no doubt. It was a gold coin, lying there amid the seashells on Gombi Island. The fisherman stooped to pick it up, barely able to believe his good fortune.

He had always dreamed of finding gold—the gold that pirates once buried on islands along the Louisiana coast. But never before had he found a single doubloon.

He dropped to his knees and began to rake through the shells with his fingers. He scooped them up with a flat piece of driftwood. He kicked them aside with his feet. But all that afternoon he found no more gold.

Surely the coin was a good omen. Pirates had once lurked here. The fisherman raced to the center of the island to see if he could find twin oaks—landmarks the pirates favored when burying treasure.

When he finally spotted twin trees, he was so excited he

wanted to dig with his bare hands. But he needed a shovel, so he pushed his boat into the water and rowed home with the day's catch. He would hurry back after supper.

His wife tried to dissuade him. "You'll get hurt," she said. "Pirate ghosts hate to give up their treasure."

"Ghosts? You know I don't believe in ghosts."

She gripped his arm. "They'll addle your wits. Once you see them, you'll never be the same again."

But he didn't listen. He kissed her good-bye, grabbed his shovel, and rowed across the silent waters. A full moon left a silvery path on the waves, leading directly to Gombi Island.

The fisherman pulled his boat well onto the beach and walked through the woods to the spot where he had seen the twin oaks. And that's where he started to dig. The sand was soft and dry. But he had dug down no more than a foot or two when he heard a startling noise. It sounded like something wooden being dragged across sand and seashells. The sound came from the very beach where he had left his boat.

He raced back and found the boat floating out to sea. He waded into the water and hauled it ashore. This time he pulled it even farther up the beach. Then he returned to the hole he was digging.

What hole? His shovel was where he left it, but the sand beside it was level again, as if he hadn't taken out a single scoop.

He tried to reassure himself. A big wave must have rolled up the beach and pulled his boat down to the water—and perhaps the sand was so soft it had just slid back into the hole.

The fisherman started to dig again. The sand seemed to be staying where he threw it, but the work grew harder. He stepped down into the hole and threw the sand over his shoulder. His arms were aching and he was breathing fast. Then he heard the trees swaying overhead, even though there was no wind, and he felt the earth tremble. A few grains of sand came tumbling into the hole. What if all the sand slid over him? He was about to jump out when his shovel clanged against something—metal against metal.

The fisherman threw down his shovel and began to push the sand aside with his hands. There at the bottom of the hole was a metal box.

At that very moment, something wet splashed on his head. He looked up and cried out in terror, for there above him, leaning over the hole, were three fearsome pirates. Seaweed streamed from their shoulders and shrimp crawled through their hair. The daggers they held high were dripping. Dripping what? Blood or seawater?

The fisherman didn't know which.

Drop by drop it fell on him, salty and warm. He was trapped at the bottom of that hole, shuddering and desperate. What if they decided to bury him alive?

He sank to his knees and prayed. He vowed he would

never search for pirate treasure again if only he could escape with his life. When he looked up, he saw the pirates melt into mist before his very eyes.

He leaped out of that hole. Even before he had hurtled through the woods to the beach, he heard the sound of sand sliding back into the hole. He was gasping for breath, but he managed to drag his boat down to the water.

Just as he jumped aboard, he saw that he wasn't alone.

Another pirate had materialized at the back of the boat. This pirate was twice as big and twice as fierce as the others. He too had seaweed streaming down his shoulders and shrimp crawling through his hair. And two huge sea turtles were dangling from his ears like monstrous earrings.

This pirate carried no dagger. What he held was far worse—a great, curved cutlass, dripping whatever those daggers had dripped. The pirate slashed that cutlass just inches from the fisherman's nose, spraying his face with something that smelled very much like blood. In the moonlight, the fisherman couldn't be sure.

But when the pirate pointed that cutlass first to one oar and then to the other, the fisherman began to row as if his life depended on it. And when the pirate pointed that cutlass out to sea, the fisherman rowed exactly where the pirate pointed, pulling on those oars with the strength of a dozen men.

Hour after hour the fisherman rowed, until he was afraid he would never see land again. He was sure his end had

come. He would never see his friends again, nor his wife—
his wise, wise wife.

He was so exhausted he could hardly think, but he
began to mumble the same prayer he had said when he
was deep in the sandy hole.

And lo and behold, the pirate slid silently over the edge
of the boat and down beneath the waves.

The fisherman's hair stood on end, for not one bubble

arose from the spot where the pirate sank. This pirate was a ghost, and so were the others. He immediately swung the boat around and rowed back home, too frightened to rest his aching arms.

When he was back on land at last, walking to his front door, he saw a terrifying sight. Jammed into the dirt by the doorway was the very shovel he had left on the island, and down that shovel streamed seaweed and shrimp. The fish-

97

erman wanted to fling it far from the house, but no matter how desperately he tugged, he couldn't tear it free. Somehow the ghosts had made sure he would never use that shovel to dig for pirate treasure again.

Then he noticed the door to his house was ajar and saw four sets of wet footprints leading inside. He threw open the door and saw a wild-eyed woman sitting by the fire, shredding seaweed. His wife screamed when she saw him, and he screamed, too. For the ghosts had so addled their wits that neither one recognized the other.

The Black Snake

Three merchants sailed from Persia in fair weather. They had no reason to suspect trouble. For years their ship had carried them safely to distant lands where they traded fine rugs for leather, wool, and silk.

But on this voyage a great storm arose when the ship reached the heart of the sea. Howling winds tore at the sails and huge waves swept across the deck. The merchants clutched ropes and railings, praying they would not be swept overboard. But the storm grew worse.

Suddenly a gigantic wave slammed into the ship, splitting it in two and sinking it. But a beam miraculously rose up from the wreckage, and the three merchants clung to it with all their strength. For two days and two nights they hung on, neither eating nor drinking, and at every moment they saw death before their eyes.

On the third day they saw an island in the distance and their hopes rose. They drifted toward it and soon they managed to touch the ocean floor with their feet. They dragged themselves ashore and stumbled up the beach. There they slept for hours, and when they awoke they thanked God for saving them from drowning.

The merchants began to search the island for food and water. They had little strength, but they struggled up a hill, their feet sinking into the soft sand. They felt like collapsing, until they saw what was on the other side—a castle stood on the far shore of the island.

They hurried down the hill and knocked on the door. But no one answered. So they drank from the clear stream that flowed past the castle and ate figs from the trees that lined its banks.

Then they sat down to wait. Perhaps the owner of the castle would return soon or a ship would sail by. But for days nothing appeared. And when it did, they wished it hadn't.

Far out on the horizon they saw something indescribable coming toward them. At first they thought it was a sea serpent, but soon they realized it was a gigantic horse and rider rising out of the waves.

The merchants were terrified. But it was too late to hide, for the horse was as swift as the wind.

The moment the giant reached the castle, he jumped off the horse and grasped his sword. "How dare you land on my island!" he bellowed.

The merchants told him they were shipwrecked, but the giant only scowled. "Follow me," he said. And he led all three to the depths of the castle cellar. There he handed them shovels and told them to dig three pits, "deep enough for you to stand in with only your heads above ground." The merchants were shaking with fear, but they dug the pits because they had no choice.

When they finished, the giant ordered them to put down the shovels and stand in the pits with their arms down at their sides.) Then he dumped great handfuls of sand around them and packed it tight. Within minutes, the merchants' bodies were trapped underground, except for their heads.

And then, when the merchants thought nothing worse could possibly happen, the giant let loose an enormous black snake. It circled the room three times, then slithered directly toward the first merchant.

When it reached him, it bit his lip and began to suck his blood. The merchant almost fainted, and the others were petrified, wondering when their time would come.

When the eyes of the first merchant closed and his head fell to one side, the giant laughed and left the cellar.

The snake again circled the room three times and slithered toward the second merchant. All he could do was

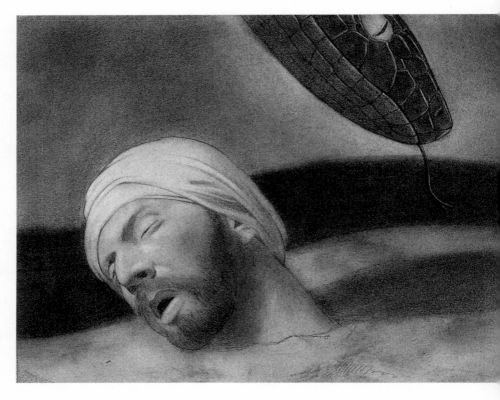

watch in horror as it bit his lip and sucked his life right out
of him.

The third merchant watched the snake circling the room
again, and suddenly he had an idea. When the snake slithered up to him, the merchant opened his mouth wide and
bit the snake with all his strength. The snake tried to free
itself, lashing its tail from side to side until the ground in
which the merchant was buried began to loosen. Within
moments the merchant was able to work one arm free. He
grasped the snake and was pulled right out of the pit. The

snake tried to wrap itself around him, but he grabbed a shovel and chopped the snake to bits.

He listened for the giant but didn't hear a sound, so he quickly buried his dead friends and slipped up the stairs. He opened the front door and was horrified to see that same indescribable form on the horizon.

The giant was returning.

The merchant climbed the nearest fig tree and hid in its uppermost branches. Moments later, the giant tied his horse to that very tree.

103

The merchant listened to the giant stomp down to the cellar, bellow, and race back up again. His footsteps echoed from room to room as he searched for the third merchant, and his sword sang as he slashed the air.

But when he couldn't find him he went outside to rest beneath the fig tree.

The merchant waited until the giant began to snore. Then, holding his breath, he climbed down, grabbed the sword, and plunged it into the giant's heart. For one terrifying moment the giant opened his eyes. Then he died—and the merchant cut off his head for good measure.

The merchant didn't want to stay on that terrible island for another minute. So he mounted the giant's horse and directed it to swim back to Persia. Once he reached home, he never set sail again.

But as long as he lived, the fear of snakes tormented him. He imagined them lurking under every bush and tree, under every rug and chair. And when the night wind whispered through the leaves, he dreamed of huge black snakes slithering into his bed.

The Hand of Death

A young man put on his finest clothes and his broad-brimmed hat and tucked a dagger beneath his belt. Then he stepped into the street and made his way through the bustling crowds of the city, cursing anyone who blocked his path.

Soon he was hurrying along the road to a nearby village. He'd learned that a girl of unusual beauty lived there with her elderly uncle, the village priest. He was eager to see her.

He followed the road as it wandered between fields and over an arched stone bridge. He paused for a moment to admire his reflection in the river beneath. But fish made ripples on the surface, so he couldn't see his image. In a flash of anger he threw a rock at the fish, then grew angrier still when the rock splashed water on his fine clothes.

He was still grumbling when he reached the village. But when he found the priest's home, his spirits rose. He leaned against the house across the way, watching until the young woman came to her window.

The rays of the setting sun cast a warm glow over the village and onto her face. He had never seen anyone so lovely, and he serenaded her with a full heart.

When he threw a red rose up to her balcony, she drew the rose inside. Its thorny stem pricked her finger but she hardly noticed the pain. Every evening he sang beneath the young woman's window, and her uncle grew worried.

He knew nothing about this young man, so he traveled to the city to see what he could discover. His fellow priests said the young man never came to the cathedral, but they had seen him gambling and drinking late into the night and arguing violently with his friends, even brandishing his dagger.

The village priest was dismayed. He hurried home and told his niece he could never approve of anyone who would bring her such unhappiness.

The next evening the young woman spoke sadly to the young man in the street below. "My uncle insists I stop seeing you," she said. She returned the last rose he had thrown to her, but he saw that its petals were glistening with her tears.

The young man was furious. Why was the old priest doing this? He returned to the city. He gambled and fought and drank until even his most reckless friends were concerned, but he could not forget the lovely young woman.

Finally he decided to return to the village to see if he could win the priest's approval. He hurried down the road, and when he was halfway across the arched stone bridge, he met the priest himself.

"I can't live without her," he cried. "I will become as righteous as the holiest of holy men."

But the priest doubted his sincerity and told him to stay away from his niece. This made the young man so angry that he pulled forth his dagger and thrust it into the priest's head, right there on the bridge. The priest fell, with the dagger still in his skull.

The young man grasped the dagger and tried to pull it out, because his insignia was on the handle for all to see. When he couldn't wrench it loose, he braced his foot against the priest's chest and pulled even harder, but the dagger stuck fast. Even in death, it seemed that the priest was victorious.

The young man was still desperately pulling on the dagger when he heard footsteps coming down the road. He

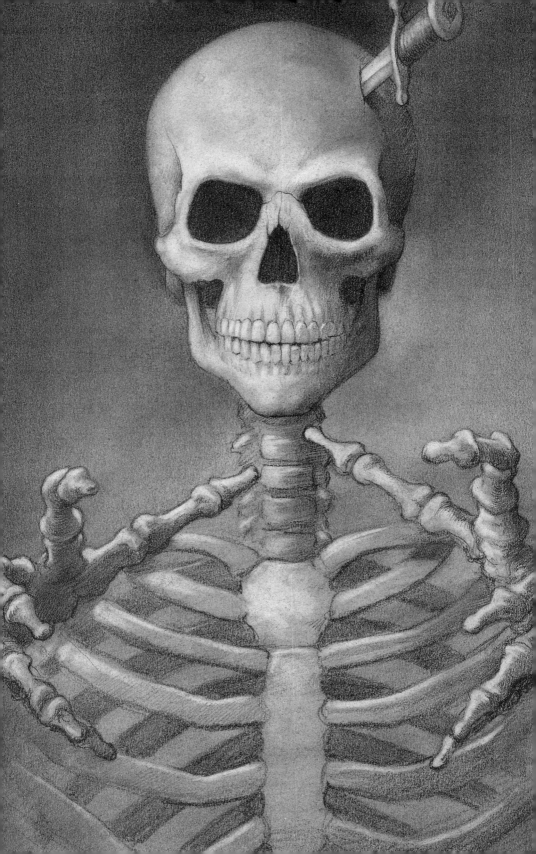

panicked and heaved the body off the bridge and into the water below. Then he rushed back to the city, terrified that the blood and water splashed on his clothes would give him away.

He hid in his house for weeks, fearing every knock on the door. But when no one came to arrest him, he began to drink and gamble with his friends again.

Months later, he decided it would be safe to visit the young woman. He hurried down the road and saw the bridge ahead. But it wasn't until he set foot upon the stones that he was struck with terror.

Standing on the bridge before him was a skeleton with a dagger sticking out of its head.

The last thing the young man ever saw was a hideous skull grinning at him, just inches from his face, and long bony fingers closing around his throat.

The Invisible Guest

Was someone following him? The baron twisted in the saddle, but he could see no one. Yet he heard hoofbeats behind him, mile after mile.

He tugged at the reins, slowing his horse so the other rider could come abreast. The hoofbeats were beside him now, but still he could see nothing.

Suddenly a voice spoke so close to his ear that he jerked his horse to a stop. "I've been looking for a comfortable castle," it said. "And I've decided to live in yours."

"What?" the baron exclaimed.

Voices out of nowhere?

Was he going mad?

He felt his horse quivering beneath him, snorting and shying to the other side of the trail.

Something *was* there!

"Well?" asked the voice. "Am I invited? I plan to move in today."

All at once the baron's fear dissolved. "What impudence!" he thundered. "*I* decide who my guests will be. And I would never entertain a guest I cannot see."

The voice turned cold. "I do not wish to reveal myself," it said. "But I can show you my power."

Suddenly a streak of lightning flew across the trail, splitting a towering oak tree and setting it ablaze. The baron's horse tried to bolt, but he held it steady. "That was an illusion," he said. "A mere trick." No sooner were the words out of his mouth than he bent over double, in intense pain.

"Is that an illusion?" the voice asked.

"No!" the baron cried.

And the pain ceased.

The baron whipped his horse. It broke into a gallop and raced for home. When they reached the castle, the baron leaped off the horse, ran inside, slammed the door, and locked it.

"That was foolish," said a voice from over his shoulder. "You can't get away from me."

The baron swung his arms through the air, frantically trying to feel what he could not see. But the voice just moved upward. It spoke from the ceiling, even more coldly than before. "I need a servant to attend to my needs," it said, "and a clean stall for my horse." The baron was dumbfounded.

"Do you want another display of my power?" asked the voice.

"No," the baron shouted. And he called for a servant.

"Take care of our guest," he told the serving girl. She looked around, confused.

"You will hear only a voice," he sputtered, "but it will make its needs known." Then he raced out the door and bellowed for the stable boy.

The girl felt gooseflesh creep up her arms. Had her master lost his mind? Then she heard laughter coming from overhead and saw two drops of slime splash on her shoe. She froze in terror.

"Be calm, you dolt," the voice said. "What your master says is true. Just be sure to serve me well."

Was it an evil spirit? She swooned and fell to the castle floor. When she awoke she saw a bucket of water sloshing itself on her face—with no hands holding it.

"Get up and dry yourself," ordered the voice. "Then get me a bowl of sweet milk with a sprinkling of fresh bread crumbs."

She set the bowl on the kitchen table, then watched, wide-eyed, while the milk and crumbs slowly disappeared. When there were but a few drops left, the bowl tipped up. There was one last slurp and the bowl settled down again, empty.

But the voice didn't eat in the kitchen for long. Soon it decided to join the girl's master in the dining hall. The baron was infuriated. He didn't want to share his table with an invisible guest.

"Show yourself," he insisted. But the voice refused. The baron's face flushed with anger. He had to know the voice's true nature.

One evening he tried scattering ashes on the hearth so he could see the voice's footprints. But the voice just blew the ashes back into the fireplace. "Don't try to trick me," it warned. "Or you will be roasted and eaten, like the pesky cook in my last castle."

The baron shuddered but continued his search. Hour after hour he looked and listened and sniffed the air for the least sign of the spirit.

He hid in the stable, watching. And when he saw a brush seeming to move through the air by itself, he knew the voice was currying its invisible horse. What he didn't see, however, was the slime dripping onto the straw.

When he heard light footsteps on the stairs, he thought the voice was coming down from its attic room. And when he caught a whiff of damp rot, he guessed the voice was nearby.

But he never was sure.

Was it lurking about, listening to every word? And what devilish tricks would it play if angered?

One day an old friend came to visit. He was distressed to see the stalwart baron slip into the room sniffing, listening, looking for a clue to the spirit's whereabouts.

"Why put up with such a troublesome guest?" the friend asked. "Tell it to leave."

The baron looked horrified. He raised his finger to his lips, trying to silence his friend. But it was too late.

When the friend left the next morning, his horse suddenly shied at something on the trail—something no mortal eye could see—and bucked its rider headfirst into a dank and smelly swamp. The friend sank deeper and deeper into the muck, as if pressed down by an invisible hand. He was never seen again.

When the baron learned that his friend's horse had returned to its stable spooked and riderless, he became desperate.

Somehow he must get rid of the evil spirit. He lay awake all that night devising a plan. He arose before dawn, shivering, and roused the stable boy. "Listen carefully," he whispered. And he gave the boy directions to a distant castle.

The boy jumped on a horse and rushed down the trail. Long after dark he returned, accompanied by the bravest knight in the land.

Hours before, the baron had heard the voice's footsteps going up the stairs to bed. He whispered to the knight, begging him not to speak or to let his armor clank against the stone steps. Then they tiptoed up to the voice's attic room.

The knight slipped in and pulled forth his sword, slashing left and right. He sliced the bedding, tipped over the chair and table, and swung his sword through every inch of empty air.

When he was sure nothing could have survived his ferocious assault, he returned to the hall, sweating and proud. "That's done," he said.

But the voice was heard once more, seeming to come from nowhere. "I'm not that easily caught," it told the knight.

"And as for you," it told the baron, "your betrayal endangers this castle and everyone in it."

The baron felt himself thrust to the very edge of oblivion. He lay motionless on the floor, dreaming he had to clamber up the slippery walls of an infinitely deep well. When he finally reached the top, he regained consciousness.

The knight had fled, chased out of the castle by his own sword. But servants were hovering nearby. And there was an unmistakable whiff of rot in the air.

The baron had to admit he was beaten. For all he knew, the invisible guest would be there until he drew his very last breath. He might as well make the best of it.

He ordered the serving girl to pour the voice's sweet milk into the finest china bowls. He made sure the voice's favorite chair was placed at the table where the voice preferred it. He accepted the voice as his constant companion. And bit by bit he worked to earn its trust.

One night the baron was lying in bed. Moonlight was streaming through the open window. "Are you still in the room?" he asked the voice.

"Yes," it responded.

"Then show yourself to me," the baron pleaded.

"No," said the voice.

"But now we are friends."

"All the more reason to conceal myself."

"Then let me touch you to see if you are real."

"No," said the voice, remembering the earlier betrayals. "You might hold on to me and not let go."

"I swear upon my honor I would not do that," said the baron.

"Upon your honor?"

"I swear to it."

The voice slowly approached the bed. "Just one quick touch," it said.

The baron reached out, found the voice's fingers and shuddered. What he felt was slimy, like strands of jelly dripping off rubbery bone.

But as ghastly as the invisible guest seemed, the baron was overwhelmed by an urge to hang on. He had broken promises before, and now he saw no other way to rid the castle of its unwelcome guest.

"Let go!" cried the voice. "For your sake if not mine."

But the baron would not release his grip. He tightened his fingers and clenched his teeth.

In the moonlight, he could not see the voice's hand. But he could see his own. And as the baron watched, the flesh on his fingers turned to jelly, then the flesh on his hand, on his arm, on his entire body. His bones felt rubbery.

Then, to his horror, he began to disappear, until all that was left of the baron, there in his bed, was a voice—a wailing, shrieking, terrified voice.

And even that began to fade—until there was nothing.

A Trace of Blood

Luke and Mattie heard their daughter scream. They were terrified. Had their master unleashed his frightful temper on Jo? She had entered the dining room only moments before, carrying a steaming bowl of gravy.

Luke rushed in and his knees began to tremble. For there on the floor lay Jo, silent and still, with a bloody cut on her temple.

"Get her out of here!" the master ordered. He leaned back in his chair, cold and unrepentant, but Luke could guess what had happened. There was a splash of gravy on the tablecloth that Jo probably had spilled. And there were flecks of fresh blood on the rib roast, its bony end a handy weapon for the infuriated plantation master.

Mattie heard Luke moan and rushed in from the

kitchen. She knelt by Jo, crying. But before they picked up their daughter, Luke mopped the blood from the floor with his handkerchief.

If the master had seen him do it, he might have guessed what Luke was planning, but maybe not. Who could tell, from merely looking at Luke, that he practiced voodoo?

By the next evening, Luke and Mattie had given their daughter a proper burial and left that terrible plantation behind.

The Civil War was over. They had been free for years, but they still had little hope for justice. So Luke made his own plans.

He bought a beef brain, nine cayenne peppers, and some black candles. Then he cut slits in the brain, poked in the fiery peppers, and lit the candles, one by one. At midnight he snuffed them out with his handkerchief, still wet with Jo's blood and his and Mattie's tears. Then he cut the handkerchief into small pieces.

The master never gave another thought to poor Jo until one evening when he glanced out the window and caught sight of someone who looked like Luke. He shouted to him, but the shadowy figure ran down the road and disappeared.

If the master had looked more carefully, he might have seen a piece of bloodstained handkerchief that the wind picked up and swirled across the yard. The family cat leaped into the air to catch it, but the master didn't notice.

He turned on his heel and headed up the stairs to his wife's bedroom. He wanted to tell her about the man on the lawn, but when he opened the door, she was whirling in circles and shrieking with laughter. When she finally stopped, she attacked her husband, hissing and spitting like a wildcat.

From that day on, the master's wife purred when she saw her children or servants, but she gave her husband no peace. She let her fingernails grow into claws and raked them across his face whenever he came near. Finally he put her in an institution, hoping that doctors might find a cure.

But as the months dragged by, the master despaired of her ever improving. He became gaunt and gray.

Everything around him reminded him of his wife, so he left his Georgia plantation and took his children to South Carolina.

All went well for a number of years. But one evening when he was standing on the second floor balcony, he heard his donkeys braying. He looked down at the barn and was startled to see the same shadowy figure he had seen in Georgia. Was that Luke digging a hole by the stable? The master raced downstairs and across the lawn, but by then the man had melted into the dark woods.

The master's old anger returned. He was so furious, he didn't even think to reach down into that hole. If he had, he would have unearthed a scrap of handkerchief, stained with blood. He ran back to the house for his dogs and his gun. He didn't want Luke or anyone else skulking around his property.

The moment he stepped into the front hall, he felt a smashing blow to his side. He steadied himself, leaning against the door frame, and saw his son on all fours, kicking at him like a donkey. The master lunged at the young man, pinned back his arms, and carried him off to his room.

The son screamed for hours. Finally his voice became so hoarse that he started braying. Day after day he lay in wait for his father—around corners, behind trees—ready to drop down on his hands and kick him with both feet.

The master spent months dodging his son and hoping that he would improve. But the braying and kicking only grew worse.

He lay awake at night, distraught. When he arose in the morning, his eyes looked dark and haunted.

He knew the doctors hadn't helped his wife. But he finally sent his son away for treatment. What else could he do?

Now only he and his daughter were left. He was sure he would go mad if he lost her. So he took her to Tennessee, traveling in the middle of the night, crossing fields and following back roads, hoping that the shadowy figure would not find them again.

But it did.

One evening the master saw someone climbing down

from the live oak tree at the bottom of the drive. He didn't know that Luke had just tucked a scrap of the bloody handkerchief into a nest high in the tree. But he did know that something terrible happened every time that person appeared. So he raced to his daughter's room to make sure she was safe. But she wasn't there.

He ran from room to room, calling her name, but he couldn't find her. He ordered his servants to saddle his horse so he could ride forth to save his missing daughter.

He opened the closet door to get his coat, and gasped. There she was, perched on a shelf, giggling. And when she finally stopped, she was cawing like a crow and flapping

her arms, trying to fly. Each day thereafter, she spent hours sitting on a branch of the live oak tree.

The master didn't need to send her away, because she was harmless. But he sobbed as he watched her flapping by.

He now knew that he couldn't escape the shadowy figure. Luke always found him, wherever he moved. Even the wind began to mock him with the voice of the dead girl.

The master prowled around his property, night and day, watching and waiting. He missed meals, forgot to change his clothes, and let his hair grow wild.

When the branches of trees rubbed together in the

wind, he heard Jo's death cry. When clouds raced across the moon, he saw shadowy figures everywhere. But no matter how carefully he aimed, his bullets never struck anything. And no one else saw what he saw or heard what he heard. He began to believe that nothing around him was real.

Then a letter arrived from the institution in Georgia. The master guessed what it said even before he slit open the envelope. His wife had died, and she had been buried in the family cemetery there.

He started off that very afternoon to visit her grave. He rode for days, and finally, one moonlit night, he reached the lonely road that led to the cemetery. He heard footsteps behind him and saw the glowing eyes of wolves in the surrounding forest, but he was sure his mind was playing tricks again.

When he found his wife's grave, he knelt beside it, his head bowed. He thought he felt a sympathetic hand on his shoulder, and he remembered his wife's gentle touch, before she went mad. By the time he looked up, he saw just what he expected—no one.

But if he had run his fingers across the back of his jacket, he would have found a scrap of bloody handkerchief clinging there.

Suddenly he felt a tremendous urge to get down on all fours. And when his eyes began to glow, he threw back his head and bayed at the moon.

The Bridal Gown

No one in the family ever went near the attic. They hoped the eerie sounds up there were made by branches scraping against the house. But they took no chances. And that was wise, for up in the attic an evil demoness awaited them.

She had been flying past the house, years before, when the mother of the family had packed her wedding gown into a wooden trunk. The demoness loved silken gowns, and when she glimpsed the wedding dress through the attic window, she wanted to try it on.

If the mother had remembered to utter the name of God when she packed her gown, there would have been no trouble, but she forgot. And in a wink, the demoness entered the trunk. The mother could not see her and closed the lid.

The Bridal Gown

The demoness found herself trapped, and she grew angrier hour by hour. After she had been imprisoned for years, her fury was colossal. She vowed that she would take possession of the very next person who tried on the gown.

The daughter of the family had been warned to stay out of the attic. She'd also been warned never, ever, to open the wooden trunk. But she didn't know why. In truth, the gown was being saved for her own wedding. And her mother believed that bad luck would haunt her daughter for the rest of her life if she saw the gown before her wedding day.

For years, the girl wondered what was in the forbidden trunk. One day when the demoness was unusually quiet, the girl slipped up the stairs and opened the attic door. There before her was the trunk, right beside the window. She knelt on the dusty floor and quietly unhooked the latches. Then she raised the lid just a crack.

Inside, she saw her mother's silk wedding gown. She pushed the lid back and ran her fingers over the soft material, marveling at the tiny stitches. It was so beautiful that it almost took her breath away.

The girl couldn't understand why her mother kept it hidden, nor could she resist taking it out of the trunk and trying it on. But she had barely pulled it over her head when suddenly she felt as if she were spinning into the depths of a dark whirlwind.

She was already feeling sick when she looked at the

gown and saw it turning to worms—creeping, crawling, slimy worms. Worms were crawling all over her body, across her shoulders, up her neck, and into her hair. She screamed.

Her mother rushed up to the attic and began crying as hysterically as her daughter. But she managed to pull off the wormy gown, run down the stairs, and cast it into the fire. The mother was still crying when she returned to the attic, but her daughter seemed strangely calm, even cold. And as the mother watched, an evil grin spread across her daughter's face, for the angry demoness had taken possession of the girl's body.

The frightened mother suspected that her daughter was possessed and ran out of the house to find a rabbi who could expel evil spirits.

When she and the rabbi returned, they found the girl pulling food from the cupboards, tossing it on the floor, and stamping on it. And all the while she bared her teeth in an evil grin.

The rabbi realized that the demoness was hunting for jam, the favorite food of demons. So he took some down from a high shelf and told the girl she could have it if she returned to the attic with them. The girl followed, licking her lips.

When she was standing in front of the trunk once more, he told her, "Close the lid most of the way, then push your little finger inside." The girl refused, for the demoness was controlling her. But when the rabbi threatened to withhold the jam, she obeyed.

At that moment, the rabbi fervently pronounced the secret name of God, and the demoness was forced out of the girl's body by way of her little finger. The girl screamed and pulled her hand away. The rabbi slammed the lid of the trunk shut, imprisoning the demoness once more.

The girl backed away, trembling, still terrified of the demoness. While her mother consoled her, the rabbi rushed to put a huge lock on the trunk. Then he hauled the trunk onto a wagon and drove it into a dark forest where he buried it as deeply as he could, covering it with dirt and heavy stones.

Even now, some say that eerie sounds rise through the earth in that dark place. Some say those sounds are no longer as muffled as they were when the trunk was first buried.

But who knows how long it takes for a wooden trunk to rot and a demoness to claw her way free?

The Greedy Man and the Goat

The old man's wife died the very day his goat disappeared. He wept. How could he pay for a decent funeral if he had no goat's milk to sell?

He trudged through the snow to his greedy neighbor's house. Perhaps he could borrow some money. But as he walked along, he saw hoofprints that seemed familiar, leading directly to his neighbor's yard. And when he knocked on the door, he smelled savory goat stew cooking over the fire.

The old man was trembling by the time his neighbor appeared. "Where's my goat?" he cried.

"What goat?" the neighbor asked. And he quickly

rubbed the back of his hand across his chin, wiping off a glob of gravy.

"My only goat," the poor man shouted. "The goat who was going to help me pay for my wife's funeral."

"Who knows what happened to your goat?" growled his neighbor. "It's not in the field with mine. And don't bother me for money. I have none to spare."

He slammed the door so quickly that he didn't hear the old man's anguished curse: "May the fate of my goat befall you."

The poor man returned home, moaning. "At least I can dig a proper grave for my wife." He picked up his tools and went to the graveyard. The ground was frozen, but he chopped it with his ax and scooped it up with his shovel, removing icy chunks of dirt. His fingers and toes ached from the cold, but he dug deeper and deeper into the earth.

Just as the sun was about to set, he noticed something round at the bottom of the hole. He pulled a pot out of the dirt and pried off the lid. And what did he find inside? Gold coins.

The old man was overjoyed. Now he could give his wife the finest funeral his village had ever seen, with a gleaming coffin and an elaborate church service.

After the funeral was over, he invited everyone to his hut for dinner, even his greedy neighbor, for the old man had begun to wonder if he had judged him too harshly.

The Greedy Man and the Goat

When the neighbor saw all the fine food and drink, the crusty bread and tempting sweets, he piled his plate high. But even as he gorged himself, he was not happy. He could not imagine where the poor man had found the money to pay for such a feast.

The neighbor continued eating until everyone else had left. Then he turned on the old man and grabbed him by the shoulders. "Where did you steal the money?" he bellowed.

"Nowhere!" cried the old man. "That would be a sin." He raced to his cupboard. "I found this pot of gold when I dug my wife's grave."

The greedy man's face flushed with anger. He could hardly stand the poor man's good fortune. He wanted that pot of gold for himself. He thought about it every day and dreamed about it every night. Finally he thought of a way to get it.

"Wife," he said, "I'm going to kill our biggest goat and skin it, horns, beard, and all. Then I want you to sew the goat skin around me."

The greedy man's wife was sure he had gone mad, so she dared not argue with him. When he brought the goatskin into the house, she ran to find her needle and thread. Stitch by stitch she sewed the skin around her husband. And when she finished, it covered every inch of his body.

The greedy man waited until everyone in the village

was asleep. Then he trotted directly to the old man's hut. He put his cloven hooves up on the windowsill, and he butted the glass with his horns. "Give me the gold," he demanded, speaking through the lips of the goat.

The old man shuddered. He thought a demon was peering through his window, an angry demon who had discovered its gold was missing from the graveyard. The old man leaped out of bed. "Take it," he cried, throwing it out the door.

The goat picked up the pot of gold with his teeth and hurried home. He butted the door open and galloped inside to find his wife.

"Help me out of this goatskin," he shouted. "It's getting tighter. It's pinching me."

His wife grabbed a knife and started cutting the stitches, but no matter how carefully she cut, blood flowed.

"*Owwwww!*" he screamed. "Stop hurting me."

She grabbed her sewing scissors and cut the stitches even more carefully than before. But still the blood spurted forth, spattering her dress and dripping on the floor.

"Tug it off!" he wept. "I can't stand being cooped up in this smelly hide." But even when she pulled and twisted and tore at the goatskin, it stuck to his body like glue.

In desperation, the greedy man galloped to the poor man's hut and flung the pot of gold on his doorstep, but still the goatskin stuck tight. Worse yet, his cries sounded more and more like those of a goat.

He raced home bleating, with a pack of dogs nipping at his heels. "Even dogs think I'm an animal," he moaned.

He tried to tell his wife, but she could no longer understand him. He shook with terror from head to tail.

The goatskin had grown onto his body. He would have horns and hooves and scraggly goat hair for the rest of his life.

"Serves you right, you greedy old man," said his wife. She put a rope around his neck and led him to the goat pen behind the barn.

When she went out to feed the goats the next morning, she could not tell one goat from another.

"What will I do?" she wondered, "when the butcher comes?"

The Evil Eye

Long ago there were two sailors who couldn't stand each other. And there they were, mates on the very same sailing ship. One was a feisty old man named Bell, better known as Ding Dong. And the other was a pesky fellow called Liverpool Jorge.

Jorge was not a superstitious man, but Ding Dong was. And that's why Ding Dong suspected the worst when he noticed that one of Jorge's eyes was blue and the other was brown. Jorge didn't tell him that one was made of glass.

Whenever Ding Dong was around, Jorge flaunted his tattoos, because he knew how much they upset the superstitious old sailor.

Ding Dong didn't mind the pictures of sea monsters en-

circling Jorge's legs, or the great dragon on his chest, or the
whales on his arms. But he feared the pictures of a sinking
ship on Jorge's back, the cats on his shoulders, and the
crowing hens on his wrists. He thought they all foretold
disaster, especially the cats, because, he said, "they carry
gales in their tails."

So what did Ding Dong do? He crossed his fingers and
spat into his hat to protect himself. He could hardly stand
to look at those tattoos. And what did Jorge do? He just
grinned and added more. Whenever the ship docked,
Jorge rushed ashore to look for tattoo artists. They decorated him with snakes and lightning bolts and more hens
and more cats.

Jorge showed them all to Ding Dong. And Ding Dong got
so upset he started whittling in his spare time, just to have
little pieces of wood he could snap in two, in hope of a
lucky break.

But Ding Dong doubted that anything could protect
him from Jorge's cat and hen tattoos. "They'll sink us yet,"
he muttered. "Mark my words." And he began watching
for a chance to shove Jorge overboard.

Jorge had almost run out of space for new tattoos. He had
just one little circle of unmarked skin left, about the size of
a silver dollar. And that circle was in the crook of his arm.

Jorge wanted his last tattoo to make Ding Dong's hair
stand on end. So he searched in port after port until he

found an artist who could tattoo a fearsome evil eye. And when Jorge lowered or raised his forearm, that eye seemed to open and close.

But Jorge wasn't happy. He wept because he could never get another tattoo. But the tattoo artist said, "Don't worry, there are lots more ways to get decorated." And he sent Jorge downstairs to the glassblower's shop to buy himself a fancy glass eye.

Jorge had never seen the kinds of eyes this glassblower made. He was a real artist. The eyes came in all colors—red, yellow, purple, green, and blue. And not one had a regular iris in its center. One had a silver star, another had a sickle moon, and yet another had a coiled snake, white with red fangs. That's the one Jorge liked best—the coiled snake in the middle of an eye of navy blue. He handed his money to the glassblower, put in his fancy new eye, and hurried back to the ship.

Ding Dong was standing on the deck, coiling a rope, so Jorge crept up from behind and put his arm in front of Ding Dong's face. Then Jorge flexed his elbow, making the tattooed eye open and close.

Ding Dong spun around and found himself staring right into Jorge's new glass eye. For a moment Ding Dong froze, his eyes wide and his mouth agape. Then he raced below to grab a lucky horseshoe from his sea chest to nail to the ship's mast.

The Evil Eye

Ding Dong was sure that Jorge was trying to bewitch him. So late that night when Jorge was sleeping, Ding Dong tried to scoop that glass eye right out of Jorge's head. And when Jorge woke up bellowing, Ding Dong threatened to hit him with a belaying pin. "There isn't room on this ship for the two of us," he shouted.

That was too much even for a prankster like Jorge. He vowed that if anyone were to jump ship, it would be Ding Dong. Jorge knew that neither his tattoos nor the snake in his new glass eye had driven Ding Dong away.

So Jorge went ashore at the very next port to look for something more powerful. And that was where he found an artist who was a magician with molten glass.

This glassblower had made ghost ships with sails like cobwebs. He'd made glass islands that looked like monsters' hands ready to drag sailors into the depths of the sea. But most astounding of all were his glass eyes.

They sat on the shelf, side by side, looking at Jorge as intently as he looked at them. But Jorge didn't want any of the ready-made ones with ravens and rats in their centers. So he told the glassblower what he needed and sat down to wait.

The glassblower lit a flame, heated the glass and blew, creating the evilest of evil eyes, layer by layer. Rings of green and purple and black encircled a little red spot in the middle. And that red spot seemed to stick out, making even the glassblower shudder. He cooled the eye and handed it to Jorge. "Never take it out and stare at it," he said. "Just wear it all the time."

Jorge paid him and rushed back to the ship. He saw Ding Dong aloft, splicing a ratline, so he climbed up the rigging himself. Then he stared at him, face to face, eye to eye.

Ding Dong nearly went mad, but he couldn't turn away. The evil eye seemed to hold him in its spell. He stared back, horrified, and then fell silently to the deck below.

Now either that evil eye scared Ding Dong into falling and he died from the fall, or that evil eye killed him outright. Jorge needed to know which. He hadn't planned to kill him.

The captain and the crew thought it was an accident, and Jorge didn't change their minds, but he couldn't sleep and he couldn't eat. He had to know if his glass eye really had that much power.

So he went down to the galley to ask the cook if he could borrow his mirror. Then he climbed up into the crow's nest at the top of the mast, the only place on the ship where he could be alone.

He held the mirror in front of his face and stared directly into his evil eye.

Some say that a monster wave hit the ship just then and that's why Jorge fell onto the deck and died. The glassblower said that it wasn't the fault of the wave at all. But

there's only one person who can tell you for sure. And that's the man who bought poor Jorge's eye, years later, from the secondhand shop where his mates sold it.

And that man with the evil eye is walking around here somewhere—right now!

Beware!

Sources

THE HAUNTED FOREST
From *Folk Tales of Central Asia*, by Amina Shah (London: The Octagon Press, 1970), pp. 109–17.

THE MURKY SECRET
From *The Doctor to the Dead: Grotesque Legends and Folk Tales of Old Charleston*, by John Bennett (Columbia: University of South Carolina Press, 1946), pp. 223–31.

NEXT-OF-KIN
From *Spanish Legendary Tales*, by S. G. C. Middlemore (1885), reprinted in *Folk Tales of All Nations*, edited by F. H. Lee (New York: Coward-McCann, Inc., 1930), pp. 895–902.

THE BLOODY FANGS
From *Japanese Fairy Tales*, by Lafcadio Hearn and others (New York: Boni and Liveright, 1918), pp. 29–35.

SOURCES

ASK THE BONES
From *A Mountain of Gems: Fairy Tales of the Peoples of the Soviet Land*, translated by Irina Zheleznova (Moscow: Raduga Publishers, 1962), pp. 184–87.

THE FOUR-FOOTED HORROR
From *Ghosts Along the Cumberland: Deathlore in the Kentucky Foothills*, by William Lynwood Montell (Knoxville: University of Tennessee Press, 1975), pp. 166–67.

BEGINNING WITH THE EARS
From the Israel Folktale Archives, no. 8335, collected by Moshe Rabi from Hannah Hadad. A variant is IFA 3380, collected by Yakov Zemertov from his mother, Juliet, of Iraq. Previously unpublished.

FIDDLING WITH FIRE
From *A Treasury of American Folklore: Stories, Ballads, and Traditions of the People*, edited by B. A. Botkin (New York: Crown Publishers, 1944), pp. 727–31. A variant is found in *A Treasury of Southern Folklore: Stories, Ballads, Traditions, and Folkways of the People of the South* edited by B. A. Botkin. (New York: Crown Publishers, 1949), pp. 538–40.

THE LAPLANDER'S DRUM
From *Demonologia; or, Natural Knowledge Revealed; Being an Exposé of Ancient and Modern Superstitions*, by I. S. F. (London: John Bumpus, 1827), pp. 338–55, 381.

SOURCES

A NIGHT OF TERROR
From *Ha-Sippur ha-Hasidi* (The Hasidic Story), by Joseph Dan (Jerusalem: Keter, 1975), pp. 229–35.

NOWHERE TO HIDE
From *Folk Tales From Russia*, translated by Olga Shartse (Moscow: Raduga Publishers, 1990), pp. 146–53. A variant is found in *Georgian Folk-Tales* by M. Wardrop, reprinted in *Folk Tales of All Nations*, edited by F. H. Lee (New York: Coward-McCann, Inc., 1930), pp. 493–96.

THE HANDKERCHIEF
From *Folktales of China* edited by Wolfram Eberhard (Chicago: University of Chicago Press, 1965), pp. 131–33.

THE MOUSETRAP
From *Icelandic Folktales and Legends* by Jacqueline Simpson (Berkeley and Los Angeles: University of California Press, 1972), pp. 169–70.

THE SPEAKING HEAD
From *Pe'er Mi-Qedoshim* (The Glory of the Holy Ones) (Lvov: 1864). Also found in *Anshei Ma'aseh* (The People of the Story).

THE DRIPPING CUTLASS
From *Gumbo Ya-Ya: A Collection of Louisiana Folk Tales*, compiled by Lyle Saxon, Edward Dreyer, and Robert Tallant (Boston: Houghton Mifflin, 1945), pp. 275–76.

SOURCES

THE BLACK SNAKE
From *Otsar ha-Ma'asiyyot* (A Treasury of Tales), Volume 5, edited by Reuven ben Ya'akov Na'ana (Jerusalem: 1961).

THE HAND OF DEATH
From *Of the Night Wind's Telling: Legends from the Valley of Mexico*, by E. Adams Davis (Norman: University of Oklahoma Press, 1946), pp. 201–6.

THE INVISIBLE GUEST
From *The Fairy Mythology, Illustrative of the Romance and Superstition of Various Countries*, by Thomas Keightley (London: George Bell & Sons, 1878), pp. 240–57.

A TRACE OF BLOOD
From *Mules and Men*, by Zora Neale Hurston (Philadelphia: J.P. Lippincott Company, 1935), pp. 290–92.

THE BRIDAL GOWN
From *Semitic Magic: Its Origins and Development*, by R. Campbell Thompson (London: Luzac & Co., 1908), pp. 71–72.

THE GREEDY MAN AND THE GOAT
From *Russian Fairy Tales*, collected by Aleksandr Afanas'ev, translated by Norbert Guterman (New York: Pantheon Books, 1945), pp. 550–52.

SOURCES

THE EVIL EYE

From *A Treasury of New England Folklore: Stories, Ballads, and Traditions of the Yankee People* edited by B. A. Botkin (New York: Crown Publishers, 1947), pp. 421–23. Reprinted from *Liverpool Jarge, Yarns,* by Halliday Witherspoon (Boston: Square Rigger Company, 1933), Yarn 10. Also from *A Sailor's Treasury: Being the Myths and Superstitions, Legends, Lore and Yarns, Cries, Epithets, and Salty Speech of the American Sailormen in the Days of Oak and Canvas,* by Frank Shay (New York: W. W. Norton & Company, Inc., 1951).

Arielle North Olson is the author of three picture books, including *Hurry Home, Grandma!* (Dutton). She reviewed children's books for the *St. Louis Post Dispatch* for twenty-six years.

Ms. Olson lives in Webster Groves, Missouri, with her husband, Clarence Olson. They are the parents of three children and the grandparents of four.

Howard Schwartz, a noted folklorist, is the author of more than twenty books for readers of all ages. His books include *Next Year in Jerusalem: 3000 Years of Jewish Stories*, winner of the national Jewish Book Award and the Aesop Award of the American Folklore Society (Viking). He teaches at the University of Missouri in St. Louis, where he lives with his wife Tsila, a calligrapher, and his three children, Shira, Nathan and Miriam.